GODS EARTH

Charlie Gardner

authorHOUSE®

AuthorHouse™ UK Ltd.
500 Avebury Boulevard
Central Milton Keynes, MK9 2BE
www.authorhouse.co.uk
Phone: 08001974150

'All characters in this publication are fictitious and any resemblance to persons living or dead is purely coincidental

©2011 Charlie Gardner. All rights reserved

No part of this book may be reproduced, stored in a retrieval system, or transmitted by any means without the written permission of the author.

First published by AuthorHouse 04/01/2011

ISBN: 978-1-4567-7651-0

Any people depicted in stock imagery provided by Thinkstock are models, and such images are being used for illustrative purposes only.
Certain stock imagery © Thinkstock.
This book is printed on acid-free paper.
Because of the dynamic nature of the Internet, any web addresses or links contained in this book may have changed since publication and may no longer be valid. The views expressed in this work are solely those of the author and do not necessarily reflect the views of the publisher, and the publisher hereby disclaims any responsibility for them.

Prologue

Although rain was falling it was a warm night. The odd light twinkled on the distant shore. The captain had no lights showing and the engine noise was barely discernible. Their course altered slightly as they made their way towards the shore.

"It will not be long and you will be ashore. You will be met by two men just after we leave the jetty and they will help you make your way towards the road."

The stranger grunted an acknowledgement, "I can't wait to get off this stinking tub you call a yacht, captain. Have one of your men bring my kit bag on deck."

"My men have work to do; you can fetch your own bag. By the time you're back on deck we will be at the jetty. I shall not hang around so you will need to disembark very quickly."

The man shrugged his shoulders and made his way below deck.

When he returned the small landing pier was very close and the sailors had brought the wooden crates that were also to be delivered on deck.

As the yacht left the landing two men appeared as if from nowhere.

Both were holding revolvers, which were pointed at him. He knew enough Spanish to know they wanted to know what he was doing there, "no habla Espanyol, habla English?"

"A little, what are you doing here?" The voice had a rough countryside accent which surprised the stranger. He would have thought they would be well spoken.

"I am here to fight. I was told you had room for men like me. I am retired captain in His Majesties army." Truth was he had been a lieutenant who had been passed over for promotion many times.

It was at this point the stranger noticed the red flashes on their jackets. He had been told he would be landed at a Nationalist stronghold. It now dawned on him that he was amidst Republicans and Communists. Oh well that shouldn't stop him benefiting from this war.

"Amigos not only have I come to fight but I have brought rifles and ammunition."

Out to sea the yacht captain was chuckling away to himself. He looked at his first mate. "bet that surprised the bastard when he found we had landed him in to the hands of the commies. They've probably shot him by now!"

<u>Book 1 War and Friendship</u>
PART 1

Chapter 1

I was ankle deep in freezing water my fingers numb with cold & with no chance of finding shelter or warmth in this hell hole. What the fuck made me think that joining in this war would be just a holiday in the sun? I asked myself. Twenty two years old & unlikely to see twenty three. I'd broken my mother's heart when I told her I was off to Spain to fight for the Republicans.

Just a couple of years or so ago I would cycle for thirty minutes from Reading where I lived and be laying in a meadow with the sun beating down or perhaps fishing on the bank of the Thames or Loddon. Sandwiches, a flask of tea, or a bottle of orange. Simple maybe, but it seemed absolutely idyllic now.

I shifted to try and lift my feet out of the mud that sucked them in to its cold depths. Looking at my compatriots I could see the life was being drawn out of them by the cold, wet surroundings.

Our patrol or what was left of it had taken shelter in a small gully as the fog started to lift to avoid skirmishing

Charlie Gardner

Nationalist troops who'd chased us from Barcelona following the collapse of Negrins' government on January the 23rd.

With the Republican army struggling, Negrin & his Ministers had fled to Figueras near the border with France. This was in complete contrast to the welcome given to us when bedraggled we marched in to Barcelona with enormous crowds cheering us, & letting us know how they appreciated our efforts in fighting for democracy in their country.

Instead of leaving in December 1938 & being welcomed back in England by more crowds including Clem Attlee & members of the Labour party, a few of us decided to fight on which is why we were now struggling to make our way back home.

With the light beginning to fail, I realised it was time to move again & avoid capture. We knew only to well the fate that would befall us should we be captured. The Nationalists were not renowned for taking prisoners, especially in open countryside like this where it could take many months before our bodies would be discovered.

Terror was part of this Godforsaken war & we were aware of atrocities committed by the Nationalists, such as the alleged murder of 2000 people who were trapped in the bullring following the invasion of Badajos. Mind you we were not angels & it was not unusual for the Catholic Church to be targeted & churches sacked & burnt & clergymen despatched to their maker. The church had sided with the Nationalists following the election of a Popular Front government in 1936.

The leftist leanings of this government frightened the church that had held sway over the populace. Social & intellectual life was defined by the church. The church had also supported the Nazis in Germany & the Italians who had done their utmost to provide Franco with arms, bombs

& seventy thousand soldiers that he had rained down upon me & my compatriots many times.

"Come on you lot on your feet, it's time we were moving unless you want to finish your days here."

Although the terrain didn't make it easy at least being on the move might warm us up a little. We were in the foothills of the Pyrenees or at least that's what they were called on the French side and I assumed it was the same for Spain. France and a way back home.

Grabbing what rifles & ammunition we had we rose to our feet, our action slowed by the stiffness in our joints & the bitter cold. Nine of us & only five fit, three with minor injuries & Joe who was probably as close to death as you could get, without actually having departed this earth.

Joe had copped his as we tried to escape from Barcelona. The injuries were internal & the fact he had hung on this long was a miracle. Mind you he was a tough Geordie who I judged to be about thirty five. By trade he was a shipyard worker.

There had been eleven of us but we had already placed two under a cairn made of stones to protect them from predators that were probably as much in need of a good meal as we were.

"Which way sarge?" asked Jack.

Sergeant! I'd done nothing spectacular to gain my rank except perhaps show an aptitude for fighting and most of all keeping myself and those around me alive. I didn't even make it as a corporal. After some fierce fighting in which I took charge after seeing our lieutenant and NCO's killed and saved our position being overrun some major told me he couldn't spare an officer till we reached our stronghold and that I was promoted sergeant.

"Well, I don't want to be stuck in this bloody ravine if we're spotted, so we'll have to gain higher ground although

Charlie Gardner

we'll have to go carefully as the climb will probably finish Joe, & before you say it, I am not leaving him here. I'd like you to scout on ahead."

"John, we all agree with you, nobody gets left behind to those murderous bastards. We'll make it out of here one way or another."

Although I had the rank we all had the experience of fighting in this terrain & since being separated from our own Number One Company, La Marseillaise Battalion, 14th International Brigade, camaraderie meant that unless an officer was around we all used first names, and we hadn't seen an officer in weeks.

We had been thrown together in a battle just west of Cordoba, Lopera, in the south. It was here on Christmas Eve in 1936 that we had learnt the harsh realities of defeat in battle, & we were transferred back to Madrid in 1937.

In February of 1937 we were involved in fighting at Jarama & later in July at Bruneti both not far outside of Madrid. From July to September we had fought at the Ebro river.

My first real experience of war had been at Lopera. Many of my compatriots just like myself were complete virgins when it came to battle & we were beaten at every turn, & our retreat was more of a rout. If I had thought of returning home at any time the feeling was strongest then. The ferocity of the fighting had initially frightened me & the sight of seeing men killed in front of me & others with limbs blown away was something I would never forget.

However gruesome the spectacle I did become inured to the carnage & later sheltering in trenches whilst shells & bombs exploded around me I found I had lost the fear that I first suffered & concentrated more on living day to day.

Jack was five foot ten inches, wiry with amazing strength for his size. He was six years older than me & my equal in most respects, although he never showed resentment that I had rank, in fact he often said he would not wish to make some of the decisions I'd had to. He came from Cornwall but I'd never really discovered what part although he often mentioned St. Austell. Fair haired and blue eyed he still carried the tan we'd had from being in the open and sun all summer.

The climb to the top of the ridge was not to steep & for most of the way there were goat tracks to follow, but in our present condition the ninety minutes it took was like you had been marching all day with only two thirty minute rests.

"Sarge, we've got to stop for Ernie & Fred to rest awhile." said Pikey, "Fred's boots are worn through & although he won't say I'm sure his feet are blistered & bleeding but because of this bloody weather, the frostbite means he can't even tell if they're his own bloody feet"

Fred was thirty six, the eldest among us. A Norfolk man he'd been a farm labourer before coming to Spain. His boots had worn out weeks ago but with size eleven feet nothing had been found on our excursions that would fit him. He was now suffering with frostbite & if we dared take the boot off, possibly gangrene, foot rot or worse would be found, and we had no way of treating it. Ernie was a year younger, a Norfolk man & farm labourer. They'd grown up together & joined up together. They were inseparable & the way things were going they would likely die together. Ernie was having trouble breathing & the higher we climbed, the worse it got.

"OK, but only for five minutes while you check him & Fred. If we are going to get out of this shithole we have got to keep moving. I know it's hard but hopefully by tomorrow we can reach Vilamur, & find somebody to help us over the border in to France."

"I know you're right sarge but ten minutes now may save an hour or more later. If I take off Fred's boots to examine his feet, I wont be able to get them back on, all I can do is find something to bind on to the sole with a bandage that may help. If he makes it to a doctor he'll lose his feet any way. I'm only postponing the inevitable"

"You've got your ten minutes, but make them count." I replied thinking to myself that I was probably hastening the death of the wounded & placing the fitter men in more danger. "Fuck it, we've all got to die sometime. I just don't want it to be here." I said quietly to myself.

Pikey carried out his running repairs on the infirm. His knowledge of medicine was better than any of us, but even that was scant. He initially worked in his fathers greengrocery business in the east end of London, but seeing no future he took up a three year nursing course, but after two years he got the call to join the International Brigade.

We set off again under a three quarter moon which in the near clear sky was a godsend for lighting our way but could be our downfall if any Nationalists were about looking for refugees & Republicans trying to reach the safety of the French border & were eagle eyed enough to spot us. At this elevation the landscape was spotted with snow but at least it had flattened out to be almost level.

To cross the border we would have to climb higher where the snow was deeper and hid numerous pitfalls if we couldn't find someone willing to guide us.

Chapter 2

Suddenly I could see Jack running in a crouched position towards me. The ground we were traversing was fairly flat with only gentle slopes and quite a few clearings amongst the trees. Walking was fairly easy as there was a covering of pine needles with few rocks.

"Hold up a minute. There're lights & a fire showing around that outcrop, about a quarter to half a mile away, it's difficult to judge in these surroundings & this light. It could be friendly but there shouldn't be a village within fifteen miles of us." He got out in between taking in gulps of air.

I called Isaac forward & told him to let every body rest for ten minutes and then advance slowly to within a couple hundred yards of the lights & wait until Jack or I came for them. Isaac had been a solicitor in civvy street, but like me was a member of the communist party. He was thirty, six feet tall & had been schooled privately.

"Right Jack, you & I had better find out what is out there. Hopefully they will be friendly we haven't got a hope if it comes to a fight."

We made our way up the track towards the lights. There did not appear to be anybody around but just to be on the safe side Jack & I took one side of the track each until we reached the area where the small hut sat in a small cleared area. It was about half an acre in size and almost egg shaped. Scrub and low rocks surrounded the hut which had a light glowing through a thin cloth curtain. The fire just outside & slightly to the left of the door was now only smouldering remnants. There was nobody in sight.

Jack & I crouched low & whispered our plan of approach.

"It may only be a shepherd, but what the hell he would be doing up here in this freezing cold I couldn't even begin to guess at. However it could be a Nationalist outpost keeping an eye on anyone trying to reach the border."

"Jack you go to the right and try to reach the hut on its blind side. I'll do the same from the left & if you get there before me wait & don't go warming your feet in those embers we'll leave our rifles here. You take the pistol & I'll use my knife. Don't forget there are only four shells in the cylinder. Take care with this moonlight, if there's anyone inside looking out we'll be easily spotted"

"OK but can I stoke the fire up before it goes out?" he nervously replied.

"Yeah & see if you can find a brew while your at it. Right, lets go & good luck."

We both moved off, keeping low & using what cover the rocks would furnish. Nervous excitement had given me inner warmth although I knew my fingers were still so numb with the cold that I would struggle to keep hold of my knife if it came to a fight.

I reached the left hand corner of the hut & put my hands under my armpits to try to get some feeling in to them. Jack hadn't reached his goal yet & although I strained, I couldn't hear any sound of his movements.

Gods Earth

It took another two or three minutes before Jacks silhouetted face showed around the corner of the hut. I signalled I was going to approach the window to adjudge who the occupants might be.

He drew the pistol & indicated he was ready to cover me if necessary. Crouching low I moved slowly towards the window taking care not to tread on anything that may give us away. Once there I crouched under the window for a half a minute to see if I could hear any movement from within. Everything was quiet except for the usual snuffling noises of bodies at rest.

I slowly raised my head until I was able to look in to the window. The flimsy piece of cloth that covered the window was either truly moth eaten or worn out muslin. There were two rifles on the table in the centre of the room, & I could see the shape of a man laid on a wooden bed. Two others appeared to be bound together back to back & were sat leaning against the far right hand corner wall. No further persons could be seen but I surmised that with two rifles another person was probably under the window out of my line of sight.

I crept on to where Jack was & told what I could see.

"Well, if we're going to surprise them, we'll have to be quick & grab those bloody rifles before they come to their senses." Jack whispered.

"I only hope there was only one other that I couldn't see & there weren't more with weapons out of sight. Beware that no one is sleeping with a pistol at their side or out of sight. Mind you if we're fast enough we should be able to rush in & cover anybody else there. The two prisoners shouldn't cause a problem but just be aware. If your ready we'll move now, I'll kick the door in, and go in first, you cover me & don't blow my bloody head off."

Charlie Gardner

My initial kick at the door only broke off part of the bottom half, as it was so rotten, so lifting my leg higher, I aimed where the latch was. The remains of the door fell inwards & Jack & I rushed in. The light was enough for us to see, but not that bright that it was able to temporarily blind us. I heard Jack crack the pistol against someone's head as I grabbed the man asleep on the bed & held my knife at his throat. Other than two others who were trussed up there was no one else to worry about.

The one I was holding struggled a little & mumbled something incomprehensible.

"Shut the fuck up" I shouted at him, "if you don't want me to slice your throat open, shut it."

"Your English!" he exclaimed, "we're English, we're friends" he shouted.

"OK, OK," I said, "but I'm not putting this knife down till I'm sure. Jack secure yours & then come over here & cover this one for me."

The other two prisoners were wide awake now & watching every move we made.

"Who are they I asked?" I asked.

"Just a couple of peasants who were here when I arrived. They say they are refugees trying to reach France, but I don't believe them."

Jack came over & I took my prisoners own belt & bound his hands behind his back.

I went over to the other two and asked who they were & what they were doing here. The man explained that he & his daughter were trying to reach France because if captured he was sure to be put to death.

The knowledge that his compatriot was his daughter, a woman, threw me slightly, as I had not seen her in the light. On looking closer I could see she was in fact a girl aged about twenty.

Gods Earth

"What are your names?" I asked.

"My name is Jesus de Molina, & this is my daughter is Isabella," he replied in almost perfect English, "I am a lawyer by profession, but I was also a party official for the Spanish Popular Front, which is enough to secure the death of myself & most likely my daughter if captured by Franco's forces."

He went on to say, "Negrin & his governments move to Figueras will not sustain & he like many others will flee to the safety of France. A shame but we are powerless against Franco's well supplied army."

"I am going to untie you, but if you make one false move, my colleague will shoot you. If your daughter doesn't understand English, tell her as well"

"I understand well enough," the daughter interjected.

As I was removing their bonds the daughter flinched each time the rope was loosened from her arms. Once free the man stood flexed his aching limbs & then offered Isabella assistance to rise.

Again his touch to her arms caused her to blench at his touch.

"Are you hurt?" I enquired.

"It is nothing," she replied, but I noticed her father look at me then turn his eyes towards the prisoner on the bed.

I went over to the bed & pulled the prisoner in to a standing position.

"Who are you?" I demanded.

"I am Captain Stuart Wilson of the Veinte Battalion," he replied, "and who may I ask are you?"

"I am Sergeant John Bristow, we were part of La Marseillaise Battalion, 14th International Brigade, but when the brigades were disbanded in September 38, we decided to stay & fight on. We are now trying to make the border before Franco takes control of the country. Why are you still here?"

"When the recall came I was in a makeshift hospital unconscious. I remained like that for seventeen days. When I was finally fit enough to walk it was too late and I decided to make for the French border and my escape. I would be grateful sergeant if you would untie my hands and return my belt."

He looked harmless enough and after telling him any false move would result in him being hurt or at worst killed, I released his hands, returned his belt and told him to sit on the bed.

He sat on the bed but watched every move I or Jack made.

"Can you explain to me captain how this young lady came to be injured?"

"She was already in that condition when we came across her and her father. I assumed that it was the wear and tear of their trek to this place. You must have discovered yourself that the going is very arduous." All the time he was looking at father and daughter as if daring them to contradict him.

"Pity I don't believe you captain. No doubt the truth will out and I hope for your sake that you had no hand in their treatment."

At that he made a move. As he came upright, he pulled me in front of him, & produced a knife, which he pressed in to my side just below the rib cage. He was shorter than me by about four inches. I'm six feet two inches in my stockinged feet; broad shouldered & with a thirty eight inch chest & weighing just over twelve stone normally, although these last few months had taken over a stone from me.

I spun to my right bringing my left elbow up to shoulder height & then swung it back sharply to the left. My elbow connected to the side of his head knocking him to his right where continuing to spin I grabbed for the wrist of his knife hand. I caught it & putting my free hand over his, I forced his hand up with the point of the knife pressing under his chin. Mad with myself because I hadn't searched him properly, I brought my right knee up to his balls which immediately put paid to any resistance. This caused his head to fall & the knife sliced from the right side of his jaw about two inches up toward his cheek.

"You bastard," he yelled at me, "I'm your senior officer & I'll see you pay for this you peasant. Attacking an officer is a court martial offence. Get me some clean water & something to wipe this blood from my face, & bandages. You will suffer for this you cretinous bastard if this has scarred me."

"First of all captain don't order me about. Your fucking lucky I didn't kill you. Pull a knife on me then claim rank, you must be a total arsehole. I don't give a tinkers cuss about your injuries & you can see to them after I have finished asking you some questions. Now tell me how you come to be here & why these two Spaniards are tied up Oh, & don't bugger me about, I quite enjoyed hitting you the first time & I might decide to have some more fun. Give me your word that you'll behave & I won't tie you to the bed, one word or action out of place you know the consequences."

"Don't you dare to give me orders sergeant; I'll have you court-martialled as soon as we are back to civilisation."

"Once we reach France captain, your rank will mean nothing, now do I have your word or shall I tie you up again? And just so you understand do not dare to give my men orders because they'll not obey you. Got that clear?"

He started to prevaricate so I gave him a short sharp jab to the solar plexus & pushed him back so he fell back on the bed.

"Now talk & tell me what I want to know."

Charlie Gardner

Gasping for breath, he went on to explain that he had been fighting with The British Battalion 15th International Brigade around Jarama & then moved on to Guadalajara where following defeat he & some survivors had fled north. It was during this passage that he met the private he was travelling with who had been with an Irish unit known as the Connolly Column. They had made the journey with various units over the past few months but were unsure who & where they came from. Like us he said they were making for France. The Irishman was called Tommy Monaghan, but he knew little else about him.

Tommy was still out cold but that suited me, he was less trouble that way & I could obtain corroboration of Wilson's story later.

Now that Jack & I had control of the situation I sent him to find the others & bring them to the hut, but leave two out there on sentry duty.

As soon as Jack returned, he & Tom searched the hut, but other than a few personal possessions packed in two small valises belonging to the Spaniards, and kitbags belonging to Wilson and Monaghan there wasn't much else. There was some stale bread & what I thought was a spiced sausage & a piece of cheese that had seen better times. There was also a small linen bag that contained some tea leaves. I asked if they belonged to the Spaniards & when they said no, they thought they were the captains, I told Reg to make a brew for all of us.

By this time Tommy was coming round & was complaining loudly about being rendered unconscious by his own bloody side. I gave him a few more minutes then, kneeling by his side, I questioned him to ratify Wilson's story. According to Tommy they had met north of Barcelona. He also mentioned that Wilson had him carry a large leather

Gods Earth

bag most of their journey, but Jack & Tom hadn't come across it in their search of the hut.

It would be getting light in two hours so after conversing with Jack, I decided we would hold up here till dusk. In the meantime he & Tom would forage for anything edible.

The day was uneventful & we sat in a group around the table. We had little to eat but the dry bread & cheese, washed down with reused tea leaves from the earlier brew, although after what we had endured for the last few days it was a feast.

Jesus told me "although I don't know the area very well, I learnt in the last village that there was a mountain pass over the border at Esteri d Aneu in the Sierra de Compirme. An old goat herder thought we may find a guide but if not he says the trick is to climb the ravine & when you reach the top go down the other side & you're in France. Told me that his goats do it all the time! Of course he never mentioned what to do with all the snow that there is around. He did say it was one of the lowest passes in the area. There's a French village the other side called Aulus & from there you can reach the small town of St Girons."

"Well," I said, "unless anybody knows a better route that's the way we'll go, although how many of us will make it, I wouldn't like to say. How do the rest of you feel about this?"

Most nodded or murmured agreement.

"Right, everybody get some sleep, we have about four hours. Isaac & I will take first guard & Tom & Tommy can spell us in two hours. Be ready to move as soon as it's dusk."

I didn't know Tommy at all but he'd slept, so pairing him with Tom seemed the best idea. Tom was steady & precise in everything he did, possibly from his training as an accountant. Of medium build & height he was as reliable as

Charlie Gardner

anyone I had ever known. Wavy brown hair and eyes he was handsome in a blokish way and probably had a way with the ladies. He'd been schooled privately and had been part of the schools cadet officer force. Although from opposite sides of society we got on really well. There was nothing snooty or supercilious about him.

He had marvellous stories to tell of his upbringing which had me spellbound at times. So different from my own schooling, courtesy of Alfred Sutton school in Reading.

Chapter 3

When Tom woke me at 15.30 I was far from ready to rise from my slumber. For once I'd slept well. The hut although crowded with all the bodies inside had provided shelter and warmth. Isaac was busying himself with making tea from last nights tea leaves. At least it would be something hot before we set off.

With the sun setting the temperature had dropped although it was probably just above freezing.

We all gathered outside, ready to move off.

"Jack will you go on ahead as usual, although I'll send Isaac to spell you in a couple of hours. Right are we all ready?"

"I just need to relieve myself," spoke out Wilson & moved out of sight behind the hut.

"OK, but be quick, I want us altogether with Tom taking the rear. I'll take the stretcher with Pikey, you others help the wounded as best as you can."

Everybody readied themselves & prepared to move and Wilson reappeared from behind the hut but this time with a leather valise in his hand. He called the Irishman to bring his kitbag over and proceeded to cram the valise inside.

Charlie Gardner

"There'd be more chance of some of us making it out of here if we were to leave the wounded at the hut for the Nationalists to find & look after," remarked Wilson.

I moved over to Wilson & stood directly in front of him.

"Wilson, I haven't yet made up my mind about you, but let me tell you now, these men have fought all over this land, & they have struggled to get this far. As a group we decided no man alive would be left here to face near certain death if caught. If I find you not pulling your weight & helping the wounded where necessary we'll have a court martial in the field, find you guilty, & hang you from the nearest tree. Do you understand? Pikey help the others, Captain Wilson is going to help me with the stretcher."

"You can't order me about & you have no authority to hold a court martial, sergeant, so don't threaten me," Wilson shouted.

I swiftly brought my knee up to his balls & he collapsed to the ground.

"If you wish to have children should you ever get back to England, don't cross me again. Now get up & take the front end of that stretcher where I can keep an eye on you."

He gingerly got to his feet, still a little weak at the knees, & prepared himself to lift the front of the stretcher.

"Move off," I instructed.

Jesus & his daughter walked with me & he told me we should reach Esterri before daybreak.

Although it was a steady climb, it was reasonably easy going. The track was wide enough to walk side by side. After seven hours we came across a narrow unmade road. Jesus informed me this would be the road to Esterri. I sent Jack on ahead to find Tom who was now scouting up front & to look for a place we could hole up in out of view of the road.

The rest of us caught up with Jack & Tom twenty minutes later.

"Pikey, do what you can for the wounded, if you need help, grab whoever you need. Jesus, can you come over here & help me decide on what action to take in the village?"

Jesus came over & we discussed the options open to us. Because the north had been a strong supporter of the Republic, he thought we would have no problem finding help to cross the border.

We rose & trekked on for a further four hours when we heard noises from behind.

"To the woods on the right. Tom, Jack, go to the left. If we have to fight we'll take them from both sides. Keep quiet & keep out of sight. If any bugger moves I will personally shoot them." I warned.

We disappeared in to the surrounding trees & rocks. It was half an hour before the sound of horse's hooves could be heard. There were six, walking slowly because of the dark, with a soldier on each. They were armed with rifles & although I couldn't see them in the poor light, they probably had side arms. We let them pass & waited another thirty minutes before taking to road again. From their robes I guessed they were Moroccan horse soldiers bought over by Franco. They were a long way from home this far north.

We waited for half an hour before moving off.

After only forty minutes we rounded a bend in the road & could see the village ahead. I called a halt & informed everyone we would find somewhere out of sight & comfortable we could wait, while Jesus would wait for daylight & go in to the village to seek help. The ground was rocky with heathers and alpines and small groups of some type of pine tree. Under the trees the layers of needles provided comfort and insulation from the cold earth.

Charlie Gardner

Whilst waiting there was a question I needed Tommy to answer regarding the two kit bags he was carrying. One was mostly empty & appeared quite light but the other was bulky & looked heavy. He explained the heavier bag wasn't his but was the Captain's. It had been his job to carry it since they met up just north of Barcelona. He had no idea what was in the bag but it was heavy.

I told everyone to settle down & get some sleep; Wilson was to take the first watch with me. We'd be relieved in two hours by Reg & Isaac. I wanted to make sure Wilson was tired enough to need his sleep when he got the chance, & I was going to make sure he didn't get any rest whilst standing watch.

After we stood down we joined the others to sleep. Wilson was snoring softly when I made my move.

"Tommy," I said softly, gently shaking his shoulder.

As he came to I told him not to make a sound.

"What do you want," he questioned.

"I need to look in Wilson's bag."

"Bejesus sarge, he'd kill me if he knew."

"Ah, but he's not going to know is he? Unless of course, you tell him."

"You've no worries there, I can't stand the bastard. If I hadn't been useful to him, I have no doubt he would have left me behind weeks ago."

"So, where's the bag?"

He went over to some scrub growing around some rocks & dragged the bag out. I undone the strapping across the top and reached in. Everything appeared to be wrapped in pieces of cloth. Unwrapping a couple of pieces I pulled out I was left staring at a heavy gold crucifix about eight inches high, & in the other package a boxed gold necklace set with what I took to be diamonds & rubies. I reckoned there to be about thirty parcels in the bag all containing what could only be loot. There were also a couple of rolls of peseta bank notes.

I replaced the items & strapped up the top of the bag, & pushed it back in to the rocks under the scrub.

"Did you know what was in there Tommy?"

"No, I bloody well did not. If I had I would have made the bastard carry his own plunder."

I left it at that & we rejoined the others to get some rest before Jesus returned.

I had slept well, for three & a half hours before Isaac woke me. Jesus was at his side.

"Give me a few minutes to gather my senses & then tell me what you have discovered. Is there any of that tea left?" I enquired & Isaac went off to find out.

He returned with a mug of lukewarm tea, no sugar, no milk.

Jesus apprized me of his adventure in the village. The soldiers we encountered early this morning were still there, but did not appear to be looking for any body in particular. On the other side of the village was a small finca & he had spoken with the farmer. Like most northerners he was sympathetic to the Republican cause & would help us cross the border, but there was a price. He wished that once we reached the border that we give him a rifle & a pistol, together with ammunition. He says we will have no need of them once we are in France. However he was not willing to take us until the soldiers had left & on previous experience that could be another day or so. The climb through a ravine along the bed of a stream would be extremely difficult. With injured it would be ten times as hard.

The good news was he had given Jesus some bread, a rabbit, & a swede. Good news but lighting a fire could be risky & we had nothing to cook the swede in.

However the farmer had told Jesus that if we looked about the hillside we would see curls of smoke rising from fires from people working outside the village. I told Isaac to have the others gather really dry wood and find somewhere away from our camp, so the rabbit could be cooked & then brought back. Jesus offered to stay with the fire, because if the soldiers did venture outside the village & investigate, as a Spaniard he should be able to bluff his way out.

The rest of the day passed without incidence & we all settled down for the night having had an abundance of two mouthfuls of rabbit each & a chunk of bread.

Chapter 4

In the morning Pikey found me to say that he didn't think Joe was going to make it through the day. His thoughts were well founded & Joe was released from his pain just after midday. How he must have suffered, mostly in silence, it was impossible to know. We scraped a shallow grave, & gathered rocks to make him a final resting place. Pikey said a few words for those that believed in an after life. I quietly thanked him for being a good mate in the times we were together & made a promise to find his parents & let them know.

With the sun going down & the temperature plummeting to below zero we bedded down for another night. At dawn Jesus slipped in to the village again, but this time he returned with a message from the farmer to make our way up the hillside through the trees to just north of Esterri where we would find a stream. There was a bridge made of two fallen trees & we were to wait there for him to find us. After the tedium of the previous day, the activity was welcome.

With no stretcher to bear the going was relatively easy although Fred was wincing with every step he took. It was three hours before the bridge was spotted & another thirty minutes to reach it. It was now 14.00 hours.

It was dark & 22.00 hours before we were surprised by the farmer, who seemed to appear from nowhere. His name was Manuel & he told us to get all the rest we could, ready to move off at first light.

His thoughts on seeing Fred were that he may not be able to manage the journey, but Fred steadfastly insisted he would make it, & if he found it to arduous he would shoot himself.

As daylight dawned we had a hot drink of coffee, & some sausage & bread that Manuel had brought with him. Manuel told us to move on through the trees, as it was simpler to enter the ravine higher up the hill. Going was slow, with the slope of the hill increasing as we gained height. The temperature was also getting noticeably colder. I reckoned we were at approximately seventeen hundred metres but we would have to ascend another six or seven hundred to cross in to France.

The ravine when we entered it varied in width between five metres & twelve metres. At the moment the bed was just a trickle of water, frozen in places, which would become a raging torrent when the snows melted. Our pace was even slower now, & our feet were getting sodden. We kept going till dusk & were all relieved to find a dry spot, where the ravine widened, to settle for the night. Some odd pieces of wood & dry scrub were found to light a fire that gave off meagre heat but did allow us to warm some rocks that we placed in our wet socks to try & dry them a little. Those that carried spare socks used them and even provided a further pair for a pal if they had them.

Tommy discreetly let me know that Wilson had spare clothes in his pack.

"Your pack seems well filled Wilson, is there nothing in there that would help one of the others?"

"I only have what I require, but I will look to see if there is anything of use."

I stood over him whilst he looked & produced a pair of socks & a vest plus a woollen jumper, threadbare with some holes snagged in it.

"Wilson you're a shit, you could've given those up without this being necessary, but no you give no thought to anyone but yourself."

He said nothing & moved away from me.

Cold & stiff, we were glad to move off in the morning. The going was getting tougher but at least we were nearing our goal. The ravine had narrowed again and we were traipsing through water. In places where it turned a corner it would suddenly widen and a large shallow pool formed. At this time of the year it was frozen, sometimes with a small trickle of water running through a fissure.

Tom who had been covering our rear came up to say he thought he had heard noises back down the ravine. He had considered it may have been animals but on reflection did not think it likely. He & Isaac were going to fall behind us & see if they could discover who might be following us. We would press on as hard as conditions allowed.

An hour or so later the cleft widened but formed a small lake that was frozen over, except in the centre where running water was visible, & completely filled the gorge. Manuel said the ice would not be thick enough to take our weight & we would have to take the goat track, about six metres up the face of the right hand escarpment. It was narrow & curved around to the right. Manuel said it would lead us out of the ravine & on to rocky ground which although dry would be covered in snow.

There were enough hand and footholds on the right bank to gain access, although getting Fred up to the track was a bit of a struggle.

Tom & Isaac chose this moment to come & tell me that the followers were soldiers, there were four of them & they were gaining on us.

"Right, Tom & Wilson will hold here & provide cover for us to get the injured on to the ledge & around the outcrop. There is a scattering of rocks about fifty metres further back that should provide you with shelter. If one of you then holds 'em off while the other gets on to the ledge then you should both be able to retreat in relative safety. Does that make sense?"

"Sounds OK,' said Tom, 'but it will still be risky trying to make it up the ledge for the second man,"

"Agreed, but the one on the ledge can lay flat & provide covering fire. It will be difficult for him to be targeted. Once your round the bend in the path you will need to move quickly to obtain cover from the rocky terrain."

Whilst we had discussed our plan the others had manhandled Ernie, Reg, & Fred on to the ledge & were making good their escape. Wishing Tom & Wilson good luck, I hurried to join them. I was just rounding the curve of the track when I heard gunfire. I looked back & could see Tom & Wilson crouched behind rocks, but not yet firing. Typical Tom, he was a big believer in Wolfes order of not firing till you could see the whites of their eyes.

The sporadic gunfire carried up the gorge whilst I quickened my pace to catch up with the others.

* * *

Gods Earth

With no more than thirty rounds between them, Tom knew every shot had to count.

The nationalists had separated so there were two each side of the stream & they were moving forward dodging from boulder to boulder whilst one provided covering fire.

Tom sighted his rifle on a rock in the stream, at a distance of a hundred yards, give or take a yard or two. That was the only cover at that point & they had to use it. He told Wilson to take their left flank & he would take the right. The enemy gathered behind the rock & then suddenly two moved out, one each side. Tom was ready, fired, & saw his man drop his rifle & fall slowly sideways in to the water. Wilson missed his man who made it to shelter & commenced to provide covering fire.

"We need to get out of here,' said Tom, 'you take to the right and get on to the track. When you're ready, I'll follow."

"OK, but it will be tough with three of them dodging around"

"I can keep them pinned down from here, & you'll have to make sure you do the same from up there. Now get moving before they sort themselves out."

He moved off & Tom fired every time one of them showed to fire.

Two of them showed at once and Tom fired at the one on his left, & saw him clutch his head & fall, unfortunately, the other made it to a cleft in the rock on his left. The soldier loosed off a shot at Wilson who was still scrabbling to gain the track. It was enough to provide Wilson with the spur he needed to hurry himself, & he almost sprang on to the track, & dropped onto his front then edged forward towards the bend in the track.

Charlie Gardner

All the time he was being shot at but because of the angle the bullets were passing over him. Wilson made it to the bend & disappeared from sight.

Tom dropped low & made it to the escarpment and started to climb. The first four metres weren't too hard but the next two were in the open.

"Wilson, are you ready?" Tom shouted, but there was no reply.

"Shit, he must have been hit. Oh well, only one thing for it."

Tom discharged three shots in quick succession & made to clamber the last two metres to safety.

Tom felt a shot hit his ear, & a moment later another in his shoulder & just managed to make the ledge & roll over. He had blood running in his left eye & he had no strength in his left shoulder. As he crawled along the path the soldier on the opposite bank had gained height. Tom noticed & got in to a crouched position to make a dash for it & as he did copped one in the leg that sent him over the edge and down on to the frozen lake where he crashed through the ice but only sank about a foot as there was no depth to the water at this point. In the cold he realised he was slipping in to a final sleep. Subconsciously he was welcoming the rest.

* * *

Wilson caught up with others, who had made good progress through the rocks & snow.

"What happened?" I asked him "& where's Tom?"

"All went well until we had to climb the ledge; I made it & was providing covering fire for Tom, when he took a shot. I stayed as long as possible but he wasn't moving. I had already got one of the bastards but he other three were gaining ground. I called to Tom but there was no reply &

the enemy were within twenty yards of him. Because they had made the ledge, I no longer had height advantage and had too withdraw. He had to be dead or very seriously injured."

I knew the ledge was the weak point in my plan & perhaps I should have left Isaac with them as well to provide more firepower.

"Join the others. We need to keep moving, not because I think the nats will come after us, but the terrain is to open, but we can't spend much time out in this cold."

Manuel came over to join me to say we were only about seven kilometres from the border, however, it would be tough going, & we still had to descend to a French village before we would find help.

He was right it was a desperate struggle & Pikey & Isaac were carrying Fred most of the way. Ernie was beginning to buckle under the effort. As the sun was setting I decided we would have to find shelter to survive. Jack found a shallow dip that was out of the wind & reasonably free of snow. We ate what remained of the stale bread & cheese & sucked snow to slake our thirst. With just one keeping watch we huddled close together under our greatcoats. Sleep was intermittent.

Stiff, cold, hungry, we were in no fit state to attack the last few kilometres.

Chapter 5

It may only have been a few kilometres & we all bust a gut to make the border, but the strain on our bodies & minds was unforgiving.

My mind kept harking back to Tom & Joe, & reminiscing on the battles we had fought together. Joe, the shipyard worker, a communist like myself, dependable & immensely strong. Always ready for chitchat, but never to badmouth anyone. He had hidden it so well that it was two days before we even realised he was badly wounded. An unsung hero.

Tom was the opposite of me, well educated, an accountant in civvy street, his parents were reasonably wealthy & his private schooling meant he had been a member of the schools cadet force, which was one of the reasons I had left him to defend our escape. He wasn't a real socialist but became involved in the brigade through his Masonic links. This secret society was totally alien to me & prior to Tom, I had no time for masons. The Catholic Church had always treated the masons as non believers & through their links to the nationalists persecuted & murdered them. I was not looking forward to meeting his parents.

"Senor Bristow, we are at the border & I must now return to my family," Manuel informed me.

"Well I'm glad you can tell the difference between this piece of mountain & any other, because I can see nothing to indicate this as a border." I replied.

"Up here there is no formal crossing, not many people cross at this point, maybe a few goats & wild animals."

"I don't disbelieve you, I am eternally grateful to you for having risked your life to get us here. It is a debt we are unable to repay."

"There is no debt. In years to come Spain will recognize the obligation she owes you & all the other foreigners who fought for her democracy, especially the many who gave their lives."

"There is just one thing before you go." I said. "Tommy, come here with that bag you're carrying. Is there any cash in it."

Suddenly Wilson moved forward to grab the bag from Tommy, but Jack stuck out a leg and sent him sprawling.

"That's my property." he shouted.

"That I doubt very much. It's more than likely that it belongs to some poor Spaniard you came across & robbed. Now, is there any cash in there Tommy?" I asked, ignoring the look of hatred on Wilson's face.

"I've no idea. I've never looked," answered Tommy.

"Well I'll look for myself," I said tipping the bag on the ground.

It was a good a time as any to find out exactly what ill gotten gains were inside.

When the individual parcels were unwrapped, it was like an Aladdin's cave. There were numerous pieces of jewellery in the form of brooches, necklaces, chains & rings, plus cash & religious items such as crucifix & goblets.

I picked up a bundle of notes & handed them to Manuel who declined saying it was stolen. I agreed but said it would be impossible to find the rightful owner & he as a Spaniard was more entitled than most. He saw the logic & said he would use it for all in his village. The remaining cash which was mostly U,S, dollars, Escudos, French Francs and a few Swiss Francs, I kept to facilitate our return to England. We gave him two of our rifles & some ammunition. I was sad to see him go when he departed for we still had a little way to go before we would find shelter.

Setting off again I could sense that Wilson was watching my every move. I had told Jack to keep an eye on the bag & make sure Wilson didn't try to snatch it.

We may have crossed the frontier but the journey was no easier & Fred had replaced Joe on the stretcher. After an hour or so it was at last evident we were descending & morale was improving. It took another two hours but our joy was unfounded when we saw a small cluster of cottages in the distance.

The locals were friendly & offered the first real hot meal we had seen in weeks & beds for the night. There was no doctor but Pikey managed to get Freds boots off but all he could do was bathe them gently in weak disinfectant. The pain had been too much for Fred & he had passed out.

Sleeping in a real bed on a full stomach was bliss. In fact when I woke in the night I had to check that I wasn't dreaming.

One of the locals was going to Erce in the morning & could give us a lift in his cart. It would knock nine kilometres off the thirty five to St Girons. He thought that if we were lucky we may get a further lift there, perhaps all the way. I learnt that since we had joined the International

Brigade that the Popular Front was no longer in power in France & the new right wing Government was not so disposed towards mercenaries as we were now called having not disbanded when ordered in September 1938.

Discussing our problems with the local mayor it was decided that our best bet was to head for Perpignan & then to a small port where we could find a British ship to take us home. It would still suit us to proceed to St Girons & then make our way eastwards to the coast.

As it happened although the French government may not have been so kindly disposed towards us, the French people that we encountered provided us with sustenance & transport all the way, including a village nurse who treated Freds feet as best she could.

We found Perpignan full of Spanish refugees & were told the easiest way to find passage to England was to head south to Port Vendres where numerous freighters on their way to England called. We had no trouble finding help to get us to the docks. After three days of waiting we found a captain willing to take us to Poole for which those of us who were able bodied would work our passage.

We were on our way home.

PART 2

Chapter 6

My hands were filthy dirty as was my face where I'd wiped sweat from my forehead.

It was now April 1939 & I'd been fortunate enough to get re-employed by Reading Gas Company as a fitter. Surprising really as they thought I was a Bolshie bastard prior to leaving to fight in Spain. During my apprenticeship I had been mated to a very good fitter called Roy Farmer who had introduced me to communism. It surprised the management that at the end of my apprenticeship I passed out as the top apprentice that year.

Life was quiet compared to the previous two years but I found it enjoyable & loved the freedom of having a pint with friends at the weekend, or having a girl on my arm for a visit to the pictures.

In my spare time I had again taken to trips on my bicycle even as far as Devon for a week's holiday. With my tent and small stove it was fun to relax with no thought of work or the turmoil that was happening in Europe.

"No more fighting for me" I thought. Little did I believe the problems in Europe & Germany in particular would soon lay lie to that thought. My thoughts drifted to the previous few weeks.

Four weeks earlier I had spoken with Joe's parents & just a week later I took the train to Chester to see Tom's mother & father.

After a lot of walking and a bus ride and some help from a postman doing his rounds I found Mannings Lane and the large house and gardens that Tom's parents owned.

They told me Tom had mentioned me in his letters home but as yet they had not received official notification of his death.

I explained as far as I could the manner of his demise, as far as I understood it, but from their reaction & what they told me I could see they were not in favour of his going to Spain in the first place.

"He had a very good position with a firm of accountants, & would have been made a partner, had he stayed." His mother told me, & then went on "and of course he had a steady girlfriend who is absolutely devastated by all of this."

"Annabel,' I said, 'he often mentioned her & always had her photograph with him."

This brought tears to his mother's eyes & she excused herself & disappeared through the door.

"This not knowing for sure has hit Mary hard. I think I've accepted his death but with no funeral, Mary is unable to do so. Still it's very good of you to come all this way, I really do appreciate it."

"We were a close bunch of lads, especially towards the end, & we all made a promise to each other, to let kinfolk know if anything untoward should happen to any of us."

"You could tell from his letters home that there was a special camaraderie between you all."

Charlie Gardner

"It's odd,' I said 'but before the brigade I would never have dreamt that I would consider a liberal, privately educated accountant a friend. Life throws together strange bedfellows. Not for one minute can I envisage that Tom would ever have entertained having a communist as a friend."

"Absolutely, but then Tom gauged people as he found them, not by social or political background. He thought very highly of you & having met you I can tell his judgement was not ill-founded."

"That's very kind of you to say so; I just wish we didn't have to meet under such circumstances."

I left them with the promise to keep in touch, although I doubted that this would be likely.

"Oh well," I thought, returning to reality, "I've kept my promise to both men but it's not something I would wish to do again."

I returned to servicing the boiler I was working on.

Trouble abounded in Europe & at the end of April the government passed the Military Training Act requiring all men between eighteen & forty one to undergo military training. Those employed in the utility companies were exempted in some cases but to be sure I registered as a conscientious objector much to the chagrin of my parents.

They had never really understood my politics & were raised in an age when King & country was everything. They weren't ashamed, just unable to comprehend.

However, I had not kept it quiet myself, & some neighbours & friends shunned me & called me a coward. Water off a ducks back to me & I ignored their comments where possible, although there had been one or two scrapes & I was now barred from my local.

In June 1940 I received my call up papers & upon refusing to go for a medical I was called before a tribunal to have my objections tested. A farce really as the JP was a retired colonel.

"Bristow, can you not wish for the opportunity to fight for the freedom & everything this country has to offer you?" he asked.

"Other than my bike, a few tools & my clothes I have nothing to fight for, & as for fighting for King & country, if he wants it so much let him join up."

My reply caused a few sniggers by others in the court, although the JP looked apoplectic.

"Well Bristow I see from the reports in front of me that you are a member of the communist party although all reports regarding your employment show you to be well thought of by your employers & I notice that you acquitted yourself well when fighting in Spain. Having considered your case I will give you the option of joining the forces or going to jail. Would you like to give me your answer now or would you like a minute or two to ponder your situation?"

"I don't wish to go to jail, so there is no choice, I'll report to Brock Barracks first thing Monday morning."

"A wise decision Mr. Bristow I am sure you will make a good soldier. Just one thing you report to the TA centre straight after this court, I think on Monday you will be a member of his majesties forces."

So it was that on the seventeenth of June I was on a train to the 217 S/L Training Regiment R.A. in Hereford.

Chapter 7

"Right you lot, today I am going to risk my life by taking you to the ranges for practice. Any one of you even thinking of discharging his rifle in my direction will feel the weight of my boot up his arse. If any of you wear glasses you will need to fetch them now so fall out."

"Sarge, I haven't got my glasses."

"Bristow you awkward little sod, what do you mean 'I haven't got my glasses?'"

"Well sarge when we arrived & were issued with kit you said that if it wasn't given to me by the army I was to pack it up & send it home. Well I'd brought the specs with me so I thought I'd better send them home."

Opening his mouth as if he were going to swallow me he bawled "you 'orrible little bastard, do you think I've got nothing better to do than wipe you lots arses for you. I'm not your fuckin' mother you gobshite. Why your fucking father couldn't keep it in his trousers instead of fathering you and giving Hitler a fucking advantage in this war I don't know. Now fuck off & report to the cookhouse & tell the corporal you're reporting to him for duties until your glasses arrive

Gods Earth

from home. Oh & you'll do the practice in your own time, now get out of my sight."

I came to attention, saluted, right turned & made of towards the cookhouse. Once round the corner I couldn't help but laugh to myself. For the next five days I peeled potatoes, carrots, & swedes, done more washing up than I had done in my life but for those five days I ate better than the rest of the company.

The cookhouse sarge & I hit it off once I'd told him what I had done.

"That is the first time I have heard of anybody getting one over on Sergeant Moore, just wait till I see him in the mess. But seriously son you're not stupid so don't pull to many stunts. The army will always beat you. If it ain't orders or rank it will be bullshit, so take my advice do your basic training & then get on with the soldiering while they have you by the short & curlies."

"I intend to sarge, it's just that it was the army wanted me not me wanting the army so I had to have my little rebellion. Thanks again for the advice sarge; I intend to show them just how good I am."

Following further attachments gunner Bristow became sapper Bristow on transfer to 21st Company TC R.E. on the seventh October in Scarborough.

It was pouring with rain when we arrived at the station, only to find we had to march the twelve miles to camp. We made it in the dark with sodden uniforms & boots. Billeted in an old village hall, I said silent thanks to whoever had the forethought to light the boiler and take the edge of the cold.

I made a small mistake that night and rested my boots on the hot water pipes overnight to dry out. Did I have trouble the next day marching & working in boots with a semi circular sole!

In March 1941 I was promoted to lance corporal, acting unpaid of course, & in May given nine days leave & travel to return to Reading. Little did I know the surprise that awaited me.

"Christ almighty I'll swing for the no good fucking bastard if I ever see him again." I yelled.

"Mind your language son, you know how your mother hates it," my father reprimanded me, 'it may be OK in barracks but not at home.'

"Yeah, sorry dad but when you hear this you'll understand what has me so riled."

I went on to explain to him. "When we were fleeing Spain I left two men to cover our escape. This arsehole, sorry, captain told me Tom had been killed & he'd had to leave him behind. It now turns out that Tom is alive & well & that bastard, sorry again, Wilson left him while he ran to save his own skin. Tom was saved by some villagers, where a local doctor tended to him. He then managed to get back to England where he spent another four months in hospital, then a further six months at home recuperating. He's still not completely recovered but is doing well"

"Well that's good news isn't it."

"I suppose so,' I replied, 'but to think that shit left him there to die just makes me fucking angry. And sorry again, for the language."

I read the letter again & decided I would try to get to Chester tomorrow & see Tom. I would drop a line to Jack & let him know the news. Jack & I had kept in touch since returning home & he was now with the Duke of Cornwall's Light Infantry, but where I had no idea. The mail would catch up with him some time.

When my mother & father were both in the room I explained to them that I was going to Chester in the morning & depending on travel I may or may not return before my leave ended.

I managed to get a train at 06.45 the next morning but with delays & unscheduled stops for troop trains going south it took until 14.00 hours before I arrived in Chester. I managed to find a bus to Hoole & the conductress told me she would give me a shout when Mannings Lane was reached.

The house was larger than I remembered the first time & I strode up the drive & entered a covered porch, which was larger than the kitchen in my mum & dads house. I tugged the large wrought iron bell pull & heard the ringing of the bell.

A tall slender woman of about thirty five wearing an apron, with a scarf in which her hair was gathered opened the door.

"Can I help you sir?" she enquired.

"Yes, I'm wondering if I may see Tom Fortescue-Browne? If he's at home" I asked.

"And your name is?"

"John Bristow, we were together in Spain."

"Step inside & I'll see if Tom is free."

She led me through to a sitting room, asked me to take a seat & then disappeared through the door.

Moments later the door swung open & Tom entered the room. He made his way toward me & I noticed he walked with a slight limp. I literally sprang from my seat took a couple of steps toward him & although he held his hand out I wrapped my arms about him & hugged him.

"Bloody hell!" Tom exclaimed, "My girlfriends don't even greet me like that."

"Maybe they're more choosey or not so happy to see you as I am. Jesus you don't know how good it is to see you

Charlie Gardner

stood there. Now you old sod give me the full story on how you managed to rise from the dead."

"OK, but lets take a seat, I've asked Mrs Rose to bring us some tea & sandwiches. I take it your hungry, oh, & before we go any further I've asked her to make a bed up for you, so no arguments you're staying here."

"Thanks, I appreciate that; I hadn't really put any thought in to where I would stay."

The housekeeper came into the room carrying a plate of sandwiches & some fruit cake.

"Tuck in, Mrs Rose makes the bread & cake herself & it's absolutely delicious. Whilst you're eating I'll let you know what happened in Spain, but this remains between you & me. I haven't told my parents the whole story in case my father tries to take some action against Wilson. I must say, I don't know what you said to my mother, but she thinks you're the bees' knees. She is even able to forgive you being a Bolshevik, which is surprising because being a true blue member of the country set she cannot forgive me, her own flesh & blood, for my liberal views."

"Good judge, your mother,' I remarked, 'now tell me about your escape."

Tom started to relate his tale to me. "After you & the others left Wilson & I in the ravine we took cover behind some rocks & waited for the Nats to appear. They came towards, two each side of the ravine, one each side moving forward while the other provided covering fire. Two reached a large boulder & I knew they were going to make a dash, one each side, for cover on the edges of the stream. I was to take one he was to take the other. It wasn't a difficult shot but he missed."

Tom took a few sips of his tea then carried on with his tale.

"Anyway I provided him with covering fire to make it on the ledge so he could reciprocate the favour. I shouted to ask if he was in position, but there was no reply. I waited awhile & shouted again, but the silence confirmed my worst fears that I was on my own. Initially I thought the bastard had been hit. The coward had made sure he saved his own skin knowing the odds were that I would be killed. My choices were to give myself up, knowing I'd be shot anyway, do my best to reach the ledge where I could either pick them off, or wait to see if you sent someone back to find me. I realised the last option wasn't an option at all because Wilson would fabricate a story to make someone returning a waste of time."

"John, eat another piece of that cake, & if you want more tea let me know & I'll give Mrs Rose a shout. She's been an absolute godsend. Comes from the east end of London & her two children were sent here as evacuees, she came to visit them just after I came home, & mother was talking to her, found she was a nurse before she married & had children, & asked her if she would like to stay here as housekeeper & help look after me. Her husband, Bill, is in the navy so he's not home that much. My first weeks home were difficult as I was still weak & had a terrible limp, but she persevered & the limp hardly shows. Mind you when I played up I felt the rough edge of her tongue, & her language would have put a navvy to shame."

"Alright, but get on with telling me what happened next."

"OK, but it's not that exciting. As I made a dash for the ledge I copped one in the shoulder & then one in the leg, in my thigh. I'd also got a nick to my ear. I rolled off the edge of the path & down on the water which was frozen. I assume the Nats left me for dead. Did they follow you?"

"No, or at least if they did, they never caught up with us."

"I passed out on the ice & no doubt would have died, but using every last ounce of remaining strength I managed to roll myself to the edge of the ravine. I thought I was as good as dead for I was lapsing in & out of consciousness. Manuel, after leaving you and the others, followed the same path down. He spotted me and somehow got me off the ice. Stripped my wet clothes of me and wrapped me in his coat and trousers. We must have looked a pretty picture when we entered the village. Him in his long johns and struggling to carry me looking like death warmed up. Poor sod was worried that after getting the rifles off you, someone would find where he had left them as he couldn't carry me and them. I drifted in & out of consciousness for about a week but when I was lucid enough to gather what & who was around me, I realised I was alive & all thanks to Manuel & the villagers. Manuel had seen Wilson telling you his story and thought that he was lying. Making his way down the ravine, he decided to see what had happened to me. Until I told him what Wilson had done, he thought I'd been shot in the fight & died. It took about another four weeks before I was mobile enough to walk and a couple of months before I could undertake a journey to get home. Manuel persuaded an old goat herder & his son to take me over the mountain to France. Once there I contacted my parents who arranged my travel home."

I told him how I found the stolen money & valuables in Wilson's bag & had given some to Manuel & the rest to Jesus & his daughter.

"I'm glad about that' he said 'I owe Manuel my life."

"Well after this war is over, I'll take you to Spain & we'll thank him properly. Hopefully some of the others will want to come to."

Gods Earth

He smiled & said "Thanks John, that will give me something to look forward to. Since coming home I've found that any friends I had have been called up. I've been rejected as unfit but I'm hopeful of finding a job at the local TA barracks either in supply or the pay corps. Any way enough of my gripes, do you fancy a walk to the pub?"

"Love to, provided you don't drink too much & I have to carry you home."

"Well, I'll go and tell Mrs Rose & then we'll be off."

The Rose & Crown was an old wood beamed hostelry. The two bars were quite small compared to what I was used to, but the beer was second to none. There were only six other people in & a couple of them had nodded to Tom in greeting. We sat in a corner by the window & I asked Tom if he had heard from Annabel since his return.

"She called round to see me a week or so after I returned, but I think she was put off by the limp." He laughed & joked "I told her it was only my leg that was affected, & not the more important bits of my body. She's the sort of girl that would feel embarrassed to attend the hunt ball with a fiancé who had a gammy leg."

"Sorry," I commiserated, "but if she was that shallow she wouldn't have been good enough for you."

"You sound just like my mother. Annabel meant an awful lot to me John but I understand how she feels & to be honest Spain taught me there is still a lot left in my life to be happy about. Just one more thing I will need to settle with Wilson if ever I find him."

"Tom, once this lot is over I will be by your side to find the bastard & settle old scores."

"Thanks John, hopefully it will not be to long before Holmes & Watson are on the trail of the dastardly Wilson."

Charlie Gardner

The next day following a breakfast with more sausage, bacon & eggs than I had seen for a long time, I made to say my farewells.

Tom's parents were there & I remarked that I was glad to see rationing had not yet reached this far north.

His mother looked at me and explained that it was difficult in the city but here in the country, life could be a little easier. They had quite a lot of land out the back of the house which used to be paddocks for the horses, but she had long given up riding. There was also a pool fed by a stream. Although overgrown she was having the gardener clear it so she could reintroduce some trout.

With a serious look in her eyes she said, "John, I am very grateful to you for coming to see Tom. Although he won't admit it he has been down. Your visit has made an amazing difference. I actually caught him smiling and yesterday when bathing he was humming a tune. That hasn't happened since he's been back."

"He'll be alright. He's made of strong stuff. He proved that in Spain. I'll be back when I can to see him again."

Mrs Fortescue – Browne smiled & said, "say good bye to Mrs Rose, she has a package for your mother. Living in the country has its advantages, our gardener has turned part of the gardens out the back in to a piggery, nothing grand but he has two sows & the local farmer provides a boar when necessary, so we have a steady supply of pig meat, some of which goes to the correct authorities & some goes to the local villagers, the local constable is partial to a bacon sandwich. We also have chickens because mark my words that eggs will soon be on ration."

Travel home was restless as I could not stop thinking of what I had learned of what happened to Tom in Spain.

Gods Earth

Quietly to myself I made the promise that if the opportunity should arise then Wilson would pay for his cowardice.

Chapter 8

When I returned to my unit in June I knew I had a decision to make. The unit had a large number of Irish in the ranks & there habit of only fetching one pail of hot water for washing & shaving was getting on my nerves. I was getting up extra early every morning to make sure I was performing my ablutions in clean water before it was dirtied with the result of the whole hut washing and shaving in it, before they rose.

The resolution wasn't difficult; I saw the M.O. & complained of ingrowing toenails & requested hospitalisation to have them removed. They were ingrowing but not causing that much pain.

On the 13th July I was admitted to Wellingborough Park Hospital & relinquished my rank of lance corporal, not that I was that worried of its loss, I thought that regaining it would be no problem. In fact whilst convalescing in my hospital blues I managed an enjoyable interlude with a ward sister. Well worth losing one stripe!

I heard from Jack whilst recovering who suggested that when this lot was over we should all get together. He was in touch with Isaac & Pikey & would propose this to them.

Gods Earth

Keeping in touch was arduous but in a disjointed way we managed.

In September 41, I was posted to Depot Battalion R.E. & in October I thought "well here we go," when embarkation leave was granted. However nothing ever came of this & I was posted to a Railway Workshop in January 42, & then in March to Woolwich Arsenal to complete a millwrights course. My run of luck of being posted to units down south ended when in July I was posted to Yorkshire where I regained my stripe & prepared for embarkation.

We boarded a train in York that slowly made its way north. We, of course, had not been told where we were going, but it was not long before the train arrived at Glasgow. None of us had served abroad & it was disconcerting to find our route from the station to the dock was lined by Red Caps.

"Bloody hell George," I remarked, "they don't mean for any of us to fuck off home & miss the boat do they."

"If they sent all these MP's they wouldn't have needed us. Only problem is they haven't got the brains to find their arse without a picture book, so they're no fucking use to anybody." He laughed at his own joke, but I knew that like all of us it was to hide his nerves.

Once on board I volunteered to stand a watch & man the guns if necessary. First time I'd volunteered for anything but I knew that when on watch I wouldn't be below decks with every other bugger spewing up & that as a rule they would bring you mugs of cocoa laced with rum.

Idly watching the horizon & sky in the wee small hours of the morning wasn't the most exciting of activities, but it saved being below decks with sweaty men, some snoring, others talking quietly amongst themselves, all of us trying not to show the fear we felt of our first time being posted overseas to a hostile environment. Most disconcerting was that we had not yet been told where we were going. Spain

Charlie Gardner

had taught me not to be frightened of the war zone but being stuck on a ship that could be bombed or torpedoed was not my idea of fun. Swimming was not my forte.

About an hour before dawn broke I had my first inkling of our destination, not specific, but it was the Med & probably North Africa. You don't pass the Rock of Gibraltar without recognising it. Well I thought, it can't be any worse than Spain.

Two days later we were under canvas in scrub & dust in Algeria. Yes it was worse than Spain, you couldn't move for bloody insects that bit & left you going mad with scratching then suffering weeping wounds that the M.O. could do little about.

I found that sprinkling a little paraffin on my beret distracted the buggers somewhat & I also dosed the seams of my blankets the same way. It put paid to smoking in bed. It would also have put paid to fraternisation with the opposite sex if there had been any within a hundred miles of us. Standing the bed legs in tins with a little paraffin also stopped the little buggers from joining you in bed for the night!

In February we had lost Benghazi & in June the Germans recaptured Tobruk.

I was working alongside George checking underground fuel tanks. They were bone dry but needed inspecting on the inside to ascertain they were not prone to leak. The heat was energy sapping & we were stripped to the waist. I'd seen desert in Spain but not like this barren landscape. Off the beaten track you disappear and never be seen again. The heat during the day was relentless and at night the cold came and chilled you to the bone.

"OK George, my turn to go down inside, you just make sure I'm not overcome by fumes."

"Righty oh, I'll top my tan up." He replied sitting down in the shade of the one ton lorry we travelled from tank to tank in & picking up his canteen for a swill of water.

We'd already done three tanks without a sniff of any leaks & I proceeded to lift the cap & descend the ladder that dropped about ten feet to the base. There were hoops every two feet with a strip of metal so that if you fell back this would help save you. About two feet from the bottom I heard an almighty boom.

"Christ almighty," I yelled out loud & with my arms, hands & feet moving as fast as they could I scrambled up the ladder taking the skin of my back, on the safety strip as I went.

I came up through the manhole cover to find George laying back against our packs idly watching the world go by.

"What the fuck is going on?" I enquired.

"Nothing, I was just enjoying the break. Why what did y….."

"Not you, you useless fucking article. Where are the fucking shells landing?"

He looked at me as if I was insane. 'Are you drunk on petrol fumes?"

"No I'm fucking not. I was almost to the bottom when there was an almighty great bang & I thought jerry had started bombing or shelling us."

Still looking at me as if I wasn't the full shilling he said "are you sure you're OK. Nothing has happened up here, I've just been lying in the sun."

I checked around me & could see there was no evidence of any action having taken place. I then stared at George to see if he was taking the piss out of me but couldn't perceive anything untoward.

He watched me glance around again & suddenly burst out laughing.

I walked over to my canteen for a drink of water. It was now that I realised that my back felt sore. I reached behind & when I brought my hand back in front I could see there was blood on it.

"Do you think I would climb out that shithole so fast if I didn't think something was going on?"

"Well other than the shitehawks flying around, there has been nothing at all happening around here."

Shitehawks were kite hawks so called because unsuspecting squaddies when receiving there meal in the open would turn around to walk away when suddenly a kite hawk would swoop down and half your rations would disappear.

"Well I don't give a shit. Get in the truck we're going back to base to get my back treated before it becomes infected."

* * *

"Bristow what are you doing back here. Aren't you supposed to be inspecting those storage tanks?"

Captain Morris was our 2 OC [second in command] for the company & often took it upon himself to spring surprise visits whilst you were out working in the field. He was liked & respected by the troops & recognised by all.

I snapped to attention, saluted & awaited its return.

"Stand easy. What's the problem?"

"Injured my back sir. The MO has dressed it & I'm just on my way back to finish the job."

He looked at me quizzically.

"Nothing serious, sir. I was in the tank when I heard an explosion but when I reached the top, skinning my back on the way up, there was absolutely nothing happening. Brown couldn't stop laughing & thought I was going mad. I just don't understand it."

He started to chuckle & explained, "When your in those tanks, if our heavy guns open up, the sound will carry through the ground & when it reaches the tank, it is amplified. If you're in the tank you'd think you were in the middle of a barrage. Carry on Bristow." And off he strode still having a quiet laugh at my expense.

By the end of November the Allies had retaken Benghazi & Tobruk & our company moved to billets in Benghazi. Most of our days were spent controlling the port & movement of supplies. Not only had the British Army been successful but so had I. I got my second stripe.

Life went on as before but working in the port had its advantages and disadvantages. It was cooler and there was often a breeze from the sea. Unfortunately the area stank

Christmas was best forgotten but at least the effort was made to get us some extra beer for the festivities. I spent the day writing letters home to mum & dad & Tom.

Chapter 9

In January 43 General Montgomery decided to resume his push for Tripoli & we were working flat out to keep him supplied with fuel for the advance.

I was called to captain Morris' office, along with sergeant Sheldon.

"We have a problem. The fuel tanker due yesterday was hit, although not sunk about 500 miles out. Monty is screaming for fuel to keep his advance moving. As you can imagine the fact we have none & the supply ship will be another day before she can dock is no excuse for holding him up. Any ideas to help solve this?"

Sheldon & I looked blankly at him.

"Thought not," he said, "still I had to give it a try. Never mind, get back to whatever you were doing."

We turned to go & had covered about a hundred yards when I said "got it."

Sheldon looked at me & said "got what Bristow, crabs, a dose of clap, what have you got?"

I turned back to the office.

"Come on sarge, we can sort this out. Lets get back to the CO's office"

"Let me get this straight corporal, you say that the pipeline out across the desert to the dump is full of petrol, & we can give that to Monty."

"Yes sir."

"Corporal, the pipe goes up & down across to the dump, & that is on an elevation about 150 feet higher than the port."

"Yes sir but that pipe is nearly three miles long & it's ten inch pipe. If we pump seawater in this end at the port, it will discharge the other end having pushed the petrol in front of it. If you give me a little time & pencil & paper I will work out the flow rate of the pump, the capacity of the pipe, how long to operate the pump before we are pumping contaminated fuel. I reckon there must be about three & a half to four thousand gallons in that pipe. If Monty can't make it to the next filling station on that then he'll have to join the infantry and go on shanks pony."

"I can't believe it but I think you've found the answer corporal. Use my office where you'll find pencil & paper, figure out the sums then come & find me over at the officer's mess."

* * *

By the end of January Monty had Tripoli in his grasp, & in May took Tunis.

In June we were in Egypt.

"Corporal, you're wanted over the adjutant's office."

I made my way over & the clerk told me to wait & I'd be called for.

"Come in sergeant," came from the other side of the door.

"There's only me, corporal Bristow here sir."

I heard Captain Morris laugh then call back, "all right then, come in sergeant Bristow."

Not sure what I had heard I pushed the connecting door open & entered, coming to halt before the desk & coming briskly to attention.

"Yes you heard me correctly Sergeant John Bristow, number 1578854. You may remove your beret & stand easy."

"Thank you, sir. May I ask why?"

"Not difficult Bristow. I informed HQ of your idea of getting fuel supplies to Monty & although it didn't win the battle it did make a difference. They were impressed enough & passed on their thanks. I need a sergeant & I need someone who can think for themselves & on their feet. You're the man. There's going to be a lot happening soon and men like you will be needed."

I didn't know what to say in reply & I think he could see that so added "I would say that I will see you at church parade on Sunday, but as I have seen you standing easy outside the church, I assume you're a non believer. Is that correct?"

"No sir I was actually a choirboy when younger, & not just for the extra money I received for weddings etcetera. I just don't believe that the same God that both we & the Germans pray to for victory is the one I read about in the bible; in fact I would say it is definitely not the biblical God at all. Even when stood outside I still sing along to the hymns & often say a little prayer, but to the God I believe in. You have seen my records, sir, so you probably know I was & still am a conscie, a republican & a communist. Given a choice I wouldn't be here fighting this war, but I wasn't given the option."

"Well I knew some of that, but not all of it. Doesn't matter to me, although some officers will take a dim view of it. All I know, is that you are a damned good soldier. You're intelligent, conscientious, you have the respect of your men & you treat them all fairly. It makes you a damned good leader. You also have a better knowledge of the practical side of this business than any officer I know which in my book makes you invaluable."

"Thank you, sir."

Chapter 10

"Do you know George, I never guessed I'd be such a well travelled man, mostly of course thanks to the British army. My old man only saw France & Belgium during the 14 to 18 but at this rate I'll see half of bloody Europe, and Africa."

"Well my old man never came back from the last lot. I never even knew him. As long as I get back I'll be happy John."

"Well if this sea gets any rougher we'll be lucky to make it to the beach."

We'd left Sousse & were circling out in the water waiting to land at Syracuse. As soon as the ramp went down the transport shot off up the beach. Our welcome was a sign written by some wag from the Eighth Army, "Disperse quickly we don't have time to bury you!"

"Oi, driver take it a bit bloody easy will you, we're being tossed about like fucking crazy in the back here," shouted a sapper.

He finally hit the road, that was no more than a dust track, and slowed slightly but only because we were now in a queue of vehicles all making for some godforsaken place inland.

We hit a snag at Primosole Bridge. Although initially we did not know what the problem was. There were three days of heavy fighting, most of it done by the 151st Brigade of 50th Division. Commonly known as The Durham Light Infantry these lads gave the German paratroops a hard time. We were back on the slopes & watched both German & our own paratroopers being dropped.

The bridge crossed the Simeto River & was of strategic importance & the fierce fighting I witnessed from our relatively safe position on the slopes was the worst I had seen. We were shelled by Jerry's' 88mm's & suffered a few casualties but nothing like those undergone at the bridge.

The next target was the airfield at Catania. The fighting did not have the savagery of the bridge & we had the addition of tanks to assist.

We managed to take the airfield at Catania & had established a camp there.

"Sergeant Bristow, you need to report to the adjutants" office, at 15.00 hours today' lieutenant West told me at parade in the morning.

"Do you know what for sir."

"No afraid not sergeant, I only get informed when one of you is killed."

I reached the office at 14.55 hours & told the clerk I was there to see Captain Morris.

"No your not sarge, we've got a new 2 IC he's come to ……."

"Come in sergeant Bristow," came an order from the captain's office.

I marched in but nearly stopped mid stride, managed to regain my thoughts & came to attention.

Charlie Gardner

"Surprised" smirked the officer behind the desk, "don't stand easy, it's so good seeing you under my command."

Even with the ugly smile I would have recognised captain Stuart Wilson anywhere.

"Pleased to see me, Bristow?"

I had got over the initial shock at seeing him three feet in front of me & replied "you don't know how much you murdering bastard. I know about Tom & I have promised him to repay you in full."

"Don't know what you mean, & mind how you speak to an officer."

"Oh, didn't you know Tom is alive & well. As for speaking to officers I have the utmost respect for most of them but you I couldn't give a shit about. You're the type of man who couldn't lead an infantry company because the first shots they fired would end in your back. You don't frighten me but I would watch yourself if you ever find that your alone somewhere 'cos I will kill you & that's a promise. You're a fucking coward who left a man to die to save his own skin. Watch your back 'cos I will get you."

He shouted for his corporal, who stepped in to the room. "Did you hear what he said to me?" he asked.

"Hear what sir?"

"Can you not hear what is said in this office, corporal?"

"Only if I listen at the door, but I was over by the window doing some filing sir."

"All right corporal, dismissed,' then looking back at me he said, 'be careful Bristow, I have the upper hand here & at the first opportunity I will have you busted to sapper & preferably thrown in the glasshouse."

I smiled at him, leaned forward to within a foot of his face & said softly "you were a shithouse when I first came across you, & you haven't changed. You're a thief and looter.

Gods Earth

I would get Tom and a few of the others to write letters confirming my story and pass it on to Major Morris, but that would be too easy. I have plans to make you regret what you did, Watch where you go at night & always make sure you have an escort. If I catch you on your own you'll regret it."

His face showed the fear I hoped it would.

Without waiting for him to dismiss me, I took a step back, saluted, turned & left his office. As I was about to leave the corporal sidled over & said "I lied, I heard just about every word said in there, but he's been here one day & I wouldn't piss on him if he was on fire."

"Cheers corp," I said, "but do us a favour and keep it to yourself."

Over the next few weeks, the jobs no one wanted always fell to my squad. Latrines, checking pipelines out in the desert, servicing our vehicles so you caked yourself in thick black oil that even after washing in petrol was difficult to remove, & little or no leave to relieve the monotony. Every time I saw Wilson around he let me know that this was only for starters.

The push continued up the eastern side of the island on dust tracks & roads, cut out the side of the mountain, but was halted, where Jerry had blasted away a section.

"Sergeant, Captain Wilson has volunteered your platoon to go forward with bridging equipment & span the ravine."

"OK corp. I'd already had an inclination this would fall to my lads. Not to worry we'll do it."

When I got there & saw the job in prospect I realised the danger involved. The gap was about twenty five feet wide & although the view to the sea below was about one hundred & fifty feet down I had no intention of showing my diving prowess, & taking a dip.

Charlie Gardner

Bringing a Bailey bridge up into position, on a narrow road, on a mountainside, trying to get it past the infantry and their equipment took over four hours & as soon as we positioned ourselves to begin, a sniper started taking pot-shots & managed to wound two of our men before I called a halt & started to rethink the task in question.

The infantry were doing there best to keep the sniper pinned down but he was well protected and had a spotter to assist him.

"George, you willing to step out there with me, & guide this bugger in to place?"

"Well I wouldn't let you do it on your own John." He rarely used my Christian name unless we were having a bit of free time chasing the girls in town so I realised he understood the danger involved.

We moved forward & told the driver to bring the bridge slowly forward, & begin to lower the bridge but watch as the cantilever began to open as George & I would be on the supports taking what cover was available.

The sniper continued but his shooting was sporadic as he searched for a clean shot that we were doing our best to deny him. It didn't take long & the crossing was soon in position. We took cover & a rest whilst others finished off & infantry continued its forward momentum.

"George you've got blood on your arm, have you been hit?"

"No it's only a nick but if you look at the inside of your right thigh about an inch or so below where your bollocks would be, if you had any, you'll notice you're the lucky one!" and could hardly stop laughing as he said it.

I looked where a bullet had gone clean through the material, "You may laugh George, but I was born with three balls & had one removed when I was fourteen. I know that

Gods Earth

somewhere in the Royal Berks Hospital in Reading I have a spare one in their stores."

"The lads have always said that while they have a purse to keep their nuts in you have a bloody great handbag & now I know why."

"That's right George & the girls love it."

As luck would have it our spell in Sicily was being terminated early. We were to be transferred to the mainland. The Germans had destroyed as much of the infrastructure as they could manage as they retreated & we were needed, to get as much as was possible, with limited spares, up & running again.

Monty had landed at Calabria & was pressing on towards Naples. The Americans under General Mark Clark landed on the west coast at Salerno & were also heading for Naples.

It was here that I had my closest look at a German. George, myself & a driver were in a one tonner & had been sent out to reconnoitre a route for a fuel pipeline. At a crossroads we had asked a redcap for the road to Andretta & followed where he pointed. After about an hour and a half of winding around the road we saw dust across a couple of fields and stopped for a closer look.

"Fucking hell, they're Jerries. Turn this fucking lorry around & let's get out of here," shouted George.

"Quick driver, I don't want to finish my war here," I ordered.

He turned the truck around & set off the way we had come.

"Faster," I shouted above the noise of the engine.

"I've got my foot through the floor now," the driver replied.

Charlie Gardner

"You'll have my foot through your arse if you don't get me out of here. When we get to those crossroads, stop 'cos I also want to kick the shit out of that redcap."

A couple of nights later I was making my way to the Sergeants Mess when I heard a familiar voice call "Sergeant Bristow hold a moment please."

I turned, came to attention & saluted "evening sir,' I rejoined, 'and may I congratulate you on your promotion."

"Stand easy sergeant. Thank you for the congratulations; it's because of men like you that I have now reached the dizzy heights of a Major. Let's go sit over there on the wall I have something to discuss with you."

We sat & he idly surveyed his surroundings before saying "I don't know what the trouble is between you & Wilson but don't think I haven't noticed what is going on. Did you know he has requested that you should be reduced to the ranks? Are you willing to discuss this with me, strictly off the record, of course?"

"I'll not deny that there is history between us but I'm not sure you would want to hear it. The day he arrived he told me he would get me any way he could. I trust you implicitly & if pressed I will tell you, but it goes back to Spain & I would rather not burden you with it."

"But why, that's what I would like to know."

"Wilson is a thief, liar & a coward, & if necessary I could prove that. I am willing to wait, if needed until after the war is over."

He smiled, looked at me & said "I think your character assessment is correct. I will not press you to relate any more of the story to me. He was not my choice for 2 IC but he has either friends in high places or was owed some favours. He engineered his move here so having learnt your side of the story I know why. The story in the mess is, he went to Spain to fight for the Nationalists but where he was landed on the coast was controlled by the communists. From what little I've heard of the man he was only there for his own benefit so switched his allegiances and joined the Republicans. However I don't know if you will be pleased but I have put an end to his plans, at least for the time being."

"Is he transferring then, sir?"

"No sergeant you are. The Americans want someone with know-how to help them in Italy. I am putting you on attachment with them for the foreseeable future."

Chapter 11

"Find Sergeant Bristow & tell him I want him here immediately. They've discovered a mine field & need it cleared as soon as & I've said I'll send someone straightaway."

"Sorry sir but sergeant Bristow left this morning to join the Americans on attachment. Do you want me to find some one else?"

"Why the hell wasn't I told of this transfer? I'd have never let that insolent bugger swan off to a cushy number with the yanks. Find Sergeant Williams, tell him to find six men & then report to a Lieutenant Cuthbertson up at section G45C & he'll give him further instructions. As soon as you've done that I want to know who arranged Bristow's move & I'll have the damned thing reversed, if he thinks he's gallivanting around Italy with some Yankee company he's got another think coming." Wilson's face was contorted with anger & glowing red as he spit the last few words out.

"Oh, the order for Sergeant Bristow's move came from Major Morris sir. He said he would inform you himself."

Gods Earth

Wilson's face dropped, "OK corporal get on with finding Williams, then get back to your work. Unless it's urgent I don't wish to be disturbed."

* * *

"Well limey what do you think of Camp White House? We have all the facilities of a five star hotel."

"This may be purgatory to you Gary but compared to what I've just left this is bloody heaven. About twice a year I can find Whiskey in our Sergeants Mess but here the stuff is on tap. We open a tin & it's either bully beef or jam. I open one here & there's a half a pound of steak in gravy."

"It's all a matter of logistics & priorities John."

"Maybe so, but yours seem to be arse about face compared to ours."

Chuckling Gary looked at me & said "I love the way you say "arse," it sounds so British. I'm gonna love working with you. I'll go home talking like an English lord."

"Where I come from I would be classed as common, or in your world from the other side of the tracks."

Gary was from Oklahoma & was the first person to greet me at the camp. The relaxed atmosphere which in a British camp would be called lack of discipline, took a while to get used to.

"John, we've got a twelve hour pass & I'm thinking of going in to Naples for some fun, are you up for it?"

"Suits me, the girls there seem really pleased to see us. I could do with some female company. However on Saturday I have a few letters to write home, I've been neglecting friends & family lately."

"Gee you sure sound like a good son, my mom would sure be proud of you."

Charlie Gardner

"Yeah, well friends & family mean a lot to me. I suppose other than your horse & a few steers there's not a lot missing you back home."

"More than that my friend I've gotta dog as well."

We sat talking for a while about back home, my job as a gasfitter & I explained how I had fought in Spain & what had happened to Tom.

"Well you've done more in your life than I have. Most of my time has been spent chasing cattle over the range on the family ranch, I had a nice life before the Japs decided to kick off. I know we all say things knowing they will never happen but after this lot is over & if you get the chance I'd like you to visit & I'll show you the delights of the U S of A."

"I'd love that Gary, & the invite is reciprocated."

We chatted a little more & then as the hour was getting late we turned in.

Life settled down to work and meeting new friends over the next three months. I'd learnt to enjoy the benefits of my attachment.

One morning Gary & I took a platoon of men to fix some railroad track that had been blown away by Jerry as he retreated.

"Hey, Gary, I've got a 48 hour pass this weekend. Do you fancy driving over to see my old mates?"

"Love to John, but with a bit of luck I ca hitch us a trip with the fly boys if they're going that way."

"Well if you can swing that I'd love it, I've never flown before. There's one other thing that I may need your help with, that tinned steak, and the peaches I'd like to take some of those together with a couple bottles of scotch."

"Sure there shouldn't be a problem with that. I'll have a word with cook."

Saturday morning at 06.45 Gary & I together with a wooden crate that was almost too heavy for the two of us to carry boarded a 'dak' as he called it. After a little more than two hours we landed just north of Bari . After agreeing to be back at the airfield at 14.30 hours the next day we managed to persuade some RAF chaps to give us a ride to my old company for a tin of steak and a tin of peaches. We kept quiet about the four bottles of scotch we had.

We were both in uniform although mine was now made of flannel rather than the coarse serge of a British uniform. I was also wearing soft brown leather shoes.

George and his platoon were out laying on a water main in the town but the guard on the gate told me that they should be finished and back to camp in about a hour. He would let George know that his mate John was on camp and would meet him in the Sergeants Mess.

Gary and I made our way to the Sergeants Mess and managed to get a beer and a cheese sandwich.

"You've known this George and these others a while have you?"

"George and I came out to Algiers together and hit it off straightaway. We've shared all the shit that jerry and the British Army could throw at us and all the comfort the young ladies could give us. We've had a few near misses with pissed off husbands and boyfriends but always lived to enjoy the next day."

"Had a good buddy myself until they started to withdraw troops and shipping them back to England. Nothing is being said but I think they're getting ready to go in to France."

"It makes sense. Hey do you hear those trucks pulling in, must be George."

"Great. I've been waiting to meet this character ever since you first told me about him."

After introductions had been made, George, Gary and myself decided to take a trip in to town to find a bar and find some female company.

Charlie Gardner

After bringing George up to date and me extolling the wonderful ways of the U.S. army, we settled in the corner of a bar with some beers. There did not appear to be any young ladies around so we made do with each others company. We were quite merry when we arrived back at the camp and after George had found us some empty bunks and blankets we were soon in the arms of Morpheus.

The next morning George went off with Gary whilst I said I was going to find some of my old platoon.

I was wandering across to the Mess when I heard the order, "arrest that man and take him to the guardhouse."

I turned to see what was going on and saw two MP's and captain Wilson a few paces behind me. I turned to continue to the mess and felt a hand take hold of my arm.

"Stand still sergeant, you're under arrest!"

"If you mean me captain you'd better know what you're doing, otherwise I'll have you for this."

"Bristow I've got you banged to rights this time. You two, cuff him and march him off to detention. I'll be along later."

With a shove in the back from a baton I was marched across the parade ground to the cells and then forcefully pushed inside.

As the door slammed shut I called the corporal over, "Word of advice corp., any more rough treatment and tomorrow when I get out of here you will both suffer four times what I do. Capiche! Ever since one of yours fucking nearly got me shot by misdirecting us behind enemy lines, I've always wondered what fucking use MP's are. If I had found him he would have been the first enemy that I killed in this war!"

The corporal looked at me not knowing whether it was bravado or I meant it. I stared back until he averted his gaze.

Chapter 12

"What the bloody hell is going on?" I demanded.

"I don't know sergeant Bristow, but I bloody well intend to get to the bottom of this."

"I didn't think this was any of your doing Major, & I am still not sure what the hell I am doing here confined to barracks when I am not strictly with this company at the moment. That bloody fool captain Wilson told me I had stolen rations from an American base to sell in the sergeants' mess. The bastard even had the gall to call me a liar & thief in front of my old friends here."

Major Morris looked perplexed & after looking me up & down for a moment or so said, "That man has been a thorn in both my side & yours since he arrived. If I hadn't been visiting the officer's mess then it could have been days or weeks before I heard about this. I have spoken with Colonel Svenson who confirmed you asked for the supplies you had on you & he will confirm in writing. You owe him John because he knew nothing about the goods being taken off base but after concurring with the quartermaster it was agreed you had asked for the whiskey & tinned goods & that they had not been stolen."

"Thank you sir, I also owe you as well for all that you've done."

"You owe me absolutely nothing John, I'm just glad to have been on hand. If any one is to thank its sergeant Brown who when he knew I was here made sure he got a message to me. Oh & your free to return your own unit as soon as you wish."

"In that case there is something I would like you to do for me sir. ….."

* * *

I was in the sergeants' mess that evening when a steward informed me that a captain Wilson wished to see me. Three or four of the other N.C.O.s accompanied me to the covered entrance to the mess where Wilson was pacing backwards & forwards awaiting my arrival.

As I approached him he asked if we could go somewhere more private.

"I don't think so,' I replied, 'there wouldn't be any point to this if we did. Say what you have to say then bugger off." I whispered in his ear.

His lips hardly moving he told me so the others wouldn't hear, "you'll pay for this you bastard."

I leaned back in close to his left ear and quietly said, "listen to me you arsehole, God didn't put me on his earth to be fucked around by the likes of you."

I took a step back & asked "yes captain, what can I do for you?"

With his face glowing red he choked out the words, "I believe I owe you an apology sergeant & I am here to say sorry for making disparaging remarks regarding your character."

Gods Earth

"Thank you captain, apology accepted, shall we shake hands?"

I stuck my hand out which he glared at & then seeing the others stood behind me gave it one quick shake, then turned & left me standing there with a grin a mile wide on my face.

I thought of the last remark I made to him and made a mental note to remember it and use it again should the opportunity arise.

Before he returned to HQ Major Morris found me to ask if everything had gone to plan the previous evening.

We had arranged that the major would tell Wilson that although charges against me had been dropped, I was charging him with defamation of character. This was a court martial offence & would not sit kindly on his service record, however the major had persuaded me to drop the charge if I received an apology in front of the men who had witnessed the offence, and if not these same men were willing to be witnesses for the prosecution. Privately Major Morris had told Wilson that if any more of his incompetent attempts to deal with me came to his attention, he would personally rip the pips of his shoulders.

Later that day I said goodbye to George, & made my way back to Bari, where I hoped to hitch a lift to "Camp White House".

Chapter 13

Inwardly I was still seething when I arrived back at camp, but knowing I had a few people to thank for getting me out the mess I had found myself in, and made my way to the QM's office. Having thanked the QM and the cook I started towards Colonel Svensons office.

"Hey sergeant, is the colonel free to see me for a couple of minutes?"

"Well I never, the criminal limey sergeant Bristow has returned to the fold. Did you bring any supplies with you?" he chuckled.

"Only the brains for this outfit," I responded, "but please I would like to see the colonel."

He started to shout through a door that was slightly ajar and a voice replied, "OK sergeant I heard, send the sergeant in."

I made my way to the door, entered, came to attention and saluted. In the typical nonchalant way of Americans my salute was returned.

Gods Earth

"Well sergeant I don't believe I've had the pleasure of your company before this."

"No colonel, and unfortunately this was not the way I would have wished for it to happen."

My first assessment of the man was he would be a straight talking man, who I knew from base chit chat had time for his men and was always ready to listen. Discipline was fair but as with lots of the U.S. bases life was lived in a far more relaxed way until it came to the time to knuckle down when suddenly it was as regimented as any British company.

"Colonel I owe you a big apology for the problem I caused. I never realised that a couple of tins of steak and a few bottles of bourbon could cause such difficulties. I would never have asked for the things if I had known what would transpire."

"Sit down sergeant, and I will let you know how little of a problem it was for me and some news you may or may not welcome."

He told me about the call he received from Major Morris who had explained that I was being set up. After he had checked with the quartermaster and cook he responded with the message that the removal of rations from his stores had been authorised. However his next piece of information was a surprise.

"In a couple of month's time this company is being sent back to England. Ostensibly it's for rest and recuperation, but it doesn't take much imagination to realise that we're building up strength ready for the push in to France. If you really want it I could make a case for retaining your services for a while longer yet, possibly till the end of this goddamned war. In any event you will be coming back to England with us, you've earned the leave. Let me know in the next few weeks how you feel about staying with us."

Charlie Gardner

Although taken aback I always knew that my attachment to the Yanks wouldn't last forever but I was amazed that Colonel Svenson would offer to try and make a case for keeping me with his outfit.

"I don't know what to say colonel, I'm glad to know I've been of help to you and I must admit I've enjoyed every second of it, I'll need time to think over your offer."

"I guess you will sergeant, and I realise this will not be an easy decision for you. I know you've kept in touch with buddies in your old unit and you have good friends here who will not want to see you go. Give it some thought and let me know. You could let me in on your secret for where you find the time to write to so many people, keep on top of the work around here and most importantly how you manage to woo so many Italian dames. Oh don't worry, I have to account for all the condoms this unit get through and when I questioned the doc he told me that you and Sergeant Cordell are culpable for damn near half the issue! No don't answer that it would probably shock me."

"Well however I decide I most definitely will not regret a moment of the time spent with you and your men colonel. I'll let you know the results of my thoughts in due course. Once again thanks for everything."

I stood, came to attention, and saluted. The usual flip of fingers off the forehead was returned and I turned and marched out.

I made my way over to the Sergeants Mess to find Gary and let him know what had been discussed in the colonel's office.

"I told you ages ago that our forces were slowly being withdrawn to bases in England and that it could only be for preparing to invade France. What I cannot comprehend is why he should wish to offer you a placement with us, goddamnit I could wup your arse any day."

Chapter 14

The two months passed quickly & having said goodbye to Gary and others, I found myself back in England, during May, on leave for four weeks. Technically I was still attached to the Americans but Colonel Svenson had told me I would not need to report back to him but would hear from Major Morris where my next posting would take me.

I managed to get a train from Paddington to Reading & as luck would have it saw an old timer friend of my fathers on the platform collecting mailbags from the train.

"Is Charlie Bristow working today?" I asked him.

"Yeah, Charlie's over at the sorting office, if you want you can ride over on the wagon with me. Sling your kitbag in with the mail."

"That would be great Frank. Thought you'd be retired by now, but I suppose with the war you've got a stay of execution."

"Bloody war! I should have been gone from here fifteen months ago, I could be on the side of some cool river bank, a bottle of beer and some sandwiches idling my time away."

Charlie Gardner

Within a few minutes we were trundling out of the station, through the bus station, across the road, and down the slope next to the Great Western Hotel and into the underground entrance of the sorting office.

"Go through the door over there and you should find your dad in the sorting office."

"Thanks Frank, give my regards to your wife." His instructions were a little surplus as I had been visiting my dad at work since I was eight years old.

"Hey old man they working you to hard?"

My father turned to see me and rejoined "harder than the life of Riley you've been living, with that Yankee bunch you were with."

I shook his hand and he told me that my mother couldn't Wait to have me home if only for a short time.

* * *

"I know I've only been home a couple of days mum but I need to see Tom, but I promise I'll only spend a couple days in Chester, then I'll be back and you can have me at home till I'm recalled. I'll even take you for a walk along the river to Sonning and buy you a tea at the White Hart. I say a couple of days but it may take a few more with all these troop trains making to the south. There's going to be big bloody push somewhere if I'm not mistaken. Whoops sorry about the cussing, I've spent to long in the army to notice it."

"That would be lovely but you must have better things to do with your time at home." This was a statement more than a question and in reality my mother would rather I spent some time with her.

I looked at her, smiled, and replied, "There's a load more things I'd like to do but until this wars over and I can call my time my own, I do what I can when I can."

"Me and your dad realise that, so don't pay no heed to what we say. We're lucky to have you home at all; some sons only make it to the nearest pub."

So it was only a day at home, forty eight hours, later I was in Chester, sat in Tom's garden, chatting over what I had been up to since we last met.

* * *

"I've been waiting for you to return. You're never going to believe who I met in Chester a few months back."

"Well," I replied, "as I don't move in the same circle of friends that you do I'll probably find it bloody impossible. Why don't you just tell me?"

"Back in January, I attended a party given by my fathers firm for clients and acquaintances. Well blow me if there weren't a couple of solicitors there, one a rather attractive young lady. I did not recognise her but as soon as she espied me, she made her excuses to some old buffers that she was engaged in conversation with and made a beeline for me. John, you will not believe this but it was that Spanish girl, Isabella."

"Bugger me do you mean the one we found in the hut in Spain when we were making for the border?" I was absolutely surprised by his news but before I could say anything else, he shushed me so he could carry on relating his news.

"Yes, that one. When I asked her what she was doing in Chester, she told me her father and herself had come to England as they were worried that should Germany over run France then they may be sent back to Spain. Her father found employment with the War Department working on translations of legal documents, but he insisted that she complete her Law studies. She'd done two years in Spain in Madrid and Liverpool Law School allowed her to complete her course although they only accepted her first year at Madrid, and she had to do extra study on English Law of which she had little knowledge. Unusual for a female to be admitted but some old lady dowager took her under her wing and twisted the university's arm. Whatever she made it and now she is a partner in a new firm with a Patrick Rice."

I started to laugh and Tom looked bemused so I explained myself.

"They sound like a school dinner company, De Molina and Rice. Said quickly it's like semolina and rice!"

Tom didn't really see the joke and thought my humour was at the level of a schoolboy.

Tom went on to explain that it was only a small practice, and not making a lot of money, but success was slowly building as women, it appeared, felt more at ease dealing with another woman.

We discussed Jesus and Isabella a while longer and then I told him of my nearly court martial and Wilson's subsequent apology.

"I would have loved to have seen Wilsons face when he had to apologise to you, have you run into him since?"

"No, but there have been times when I really wanted to. I know you tell me to forget it but I shall never forget what that bastard did to you, and has probably done to others since. Don't worry the scores that need settling are mounting up."

"Maybe so, but you've been a good friend, and I don't want you to fight my battles because you feel responsible for what happened to me. I don't blame you for Wilson's cowardice."

"Tom, I shall always feel partly to blame for what happened, I knew then that Wilson was a bastard. Look at what he stole, and possibly killed for in Spain, and the way he treated the Molina's. He would probably have killed them if we hadn't happened along. Since then he has done his best to put me in dangerous situations even to as far as trying to have me court martialled. One day I will ensure he gets his just deserts."

We continued to chat about the build up of vehicles and men, even more noticeable in the south and where my next posting maybe, until Mrs Rose appeared and told us she had laid some tea for us in the drawing room. She asked if we were able to pour for ourselves and when we said yes apologised and said she had to go find the children who had disappeared.

Compared to what I was used to, it was an absolute feast, fresh bread, jam, and home cooked ham, which I knew must have come from a rogue pig that had been discovered amongst the other pigs in the sty! There was even a fruit cake which although frugal on the fruit side had an unusual but pleasant taste and texture. Tom explained that although rationing made luxuries difficult, Mary was exceptionally inventive and by using carrots, apples and pears and plums from the orchard provided varied delights.

We were enjoying our tea when we heard shouting from outside.

"That's Mary Rose," said Tom jumping from his chair with me closely following.

"Where's it coming from?" I asked

"From the lawn. At the back. Quick it sounds as if she's in trouble."

Chapter 15

We both ran from the house, down the lawn, avoiding the vegetable plots that had been dug in to the lawn. We could see Mary frantically jumping up and down, waving her arms in the air and shouting. She was up to her waist in water in the ornamental pond. As soon as I reached her I jumped in to the water where I could see her daughter, Susan, lying face down. The pond was the size of a small lake and was stocked with trout. I was soon out of my depth and needing to swim to reach her.

Grabbing her, I rolled her over, and then putting my arm under her arms started to backstroke come sidestroke back to the bank. Tom had entered the water up to his chest and helped me get her on the grass.

Tom took control and placing her on her side and pulling her arm up over head and then again till thankfully she coughed up water. As soon as it was apparent that she

Gods Earth

was breathing we wrapped her in my jacket and as I picked her up she burst out crying.

I ran up the lawn with Tom and a distraught mother in my wake.

Once we got her in the house and laid her on a sofa she continued to cry but Tom spent some time consoling her until she stopped.

The problem was the moment she stopped Mary Rose laid in to her until I pulled her aside and told her the experience was enough to put her off playing by the pond again, without being yelled at.

Mrs Rose apologised and took young Susan upstairs for a warm bath and bed.

"I suppose we ought to go and have a bath and find some dry clothes to get in to," Tom said as Mary and Susan disappeared through the door.

"Just as well I have a spare pair of trousers and shirt with me. I wasn't expecting to go swimming this trip. Still, a hot bath would be welcome, that pond is bloody freezing!"

"Well I hope there's enough hot water for the three of us otherwise you may have found our trout pond warmer," Tom laughingly replied.

After bathing Tom and I went back to our tea which was now cold, so we went to the kitchen to boil the kettle for a fresh pot.

The last morsels of cake were just being devoured when Mrs Rose entered the room.

Throwing her arms around me and with tears in her eyes she could not stop thanking me for saving her little girl, "I've left her upstairs, sleeping. Will's back from school and is sitting by her bedside. He may be only eight but he's always been protective towards Susan. Bill always tells him he's the head of the family when he's at sea. Tells me she'll want to see him when she wakes up!"

Charlie Gardner

"It was Tom more than me. I had no idea what to do once she was back on the lawn."

"It was both of you and I shall never be able to thank you enough. How would I ever have explained to Bill if anything had happened to her? It would have knocked him sideways. He loves them both and so enjoys being with Will when he's home, but he absolutely dotes on Susan. She was that unexpected little gift as we thought I'd be unable to have another child after Will was born. But then three years later I suddenly found I was expecting again"

"Well the good news is they'll both be here for him when he gets his next leave. I mean he's been out in the south Atlantic for nearly eighteen months now. He knows he welcome here, I enjoy his company and his tales. You have all become part of an extended family for me. You got me through the worst part of my life, and the children kept me laughing when I was in despair. Nobody else wanted to play football with 'old gammy leg' but young Will never complained even though I play like a girlie!"

"Mr Tom it's us who owes you. We don't even have a house left now the jerries have bombed the east end out of existence"

"There will always be a home here for you. You're indispensable."

Chapter 16

"John, while you were in Chester a letter arrived with a U.S. forces stamp on it. Do you think you've got to go back already?"

"Maybe, but it's probably telling me of where and when I've got to report. Shouldn't worry mum, it wont be straight away."

I opened the letter to find I was to report to Aldershot in a week's time. There was no further information.

The week went fast and at the beginning of June I found myself in a RE camp just outside Aldershot waiting to see a Captain Johnson.

"You must be the luckiest soldier alive sergeant. You've missed the invasion of Europe and I've been instructed to give you fourteen days leave prior to your posting to the 23rd Field Company. I believe you've just had four weeks leave from your present attachment. Lucky for you a Colonel Svenson considers you still to be on active service and indicates you will be due leave prior to posting. Before you join the 23rd you will be helping out at Park Royal training school until December as an instructor. You will then report to the 23rd in Ismalia, which for your information is in Egypt. Any questions sergeant?"

"Yes Sir. If I am allowed to take my leave over Christmas I'd happily forgo seven days. Other than that, no questions."

* * *

So it was in January 1945 I found myself in Egypt undergoing further training prior to being sent to Palestine.

At Ismalia we were given further weapons training as Palestine was turning out to be more dangerous than the Russian front, Egypt hadn't changed since I was last there. There were still numerous British troops on the streets to maintain law and order. The "Bread and Freedom" party, which was basically the communists, held sway with a large part of the populace. The main difference was that the Bread and Freedom party were Trotskyites who didn't get on to well with the communists. Although I had sympathy with their aims I didn't get involved although many British serviceman did. Following completion of my weapons training I was on my way to Palestine.

I landed at Haifa. The moment I landed I was told to watch out for terrorists who felt no compunction whatsoever in killing British troops who were occupying their land even though they had been there for less a time than the present Palestinian inhabitants. "Fuck," I thought, "one moment I'm fighting Hitler who's oppressing the Jews and the next minute the Jews are fighting me and want to blow my brains out."

Home was a cordoned off area in the town centred around two small hotels. Not the worst billets but they

Gods Earth

became depressingly hot no matter how many windows you opened or fans you had trying to move the air.

Primarily our job was to keep the gas and oil pipelines flowing although we also had to carry out spells of guarding the camp and controlling immigration of Jews.

Jewish immigrants were a thorn in our side and most if not all were illegal's. As we caught them, they were taken away for delousing then brought back and put on a ship, usually to Cyprus. I'm sure they were back within a couple of weeks!

The gas producing company in Tel Aviv was owned by a man called David Ben Gurrion who after a few days of being around his works, I had become friendly with.

He was surprised that I was so knowledgeable about the production of gas and its distribution. Also the by products, and how to deal with them. When I told him the only thing I was looking forward to was my discharge he offered me the job as his deputy and a marvellous sounding salary and a house! He seemed astounded when I turned him down and explained that I couldn't wait to return home even if it was as a lowly gasfitter.

On the 9th August 1945 Japan surrendered and I stupidly thought that I would soon be on my way home. Wrong, the war for me was to continue.

My extended stay did however give me the chance to visit the pyramids whilst on leave in Cairo but I was more surprised when I was called in to the C.O.'s office in November 1945.

Major Walker was standing in front of his desk when I entered, "Sergeant, I think I have some good news for you. Stand at ease and I'll tell you what it is."

Not knowing what to expect but thinking he was about to tell me I was going home for demob, I was pleased with what I heard but disappointed at what I didn't hear.

Charlie Gardner

"Sergeant, the powers that be wish to offer you the opportunity to take a commission."

I was dumbfounded and mumbled, "what?"

"Forgetting the sir, I said you are being offered the chance to take a commission. Your old CO, Brigadier Morris recommended you. The war in Europe and Japan is now over and the army is looking for men to rebuild the damage it has caused. You're the type of man we need. Brigadier Morris says that although you turned down your promotion as a Warrant Officer you may accept this opening to further your career in the R E's."

"Well, I will not say I'm proud to be made such an offer sir, but as you know I never wished to be part of this army and my intention is still to be able to get out as soon as possible. I am really pleased to hear that the Major Morris I served under is now a Brigadier. He was a man I had the utmost respect for."

"Look, go away and think over your next move. I'll not reply for a day or so, so give it some thought."

For me it required very little thought. Violence was on the increase and some of my time was spent searching for arms and mines following raids on Jewish settlements. Caches were cunningly concealed below floorboards and even cellars dug under the houses, verandas or gardens.

Hotels were targeted by the planting of bombs and snipers were always a threat. Being a gasfitter back in Reading may not be the most glamorous job in the world but at least the customers weren't trying to kill you.

I had one more spot of home leave to come and decided to chat to my father about the chance to become an officer,

I took a ship from Port Said across the Mediterranean to Marseille and then up through France to Dieppe and home to England.

Gods Earth

As I thought, my father told me the decision had to be my own. My mother liked the idea of my becoming an officer but as my father said, "You get on well with your men at the moment, but they will look upon you differently once you're wearing pips, and the officers will always look upon you as someone who has come through ranks. No son, I can see you decking one or two and coming out with a dishonourable discharge."

Typical army it took only three days to get me back to Palestine although it had taken eight days for me to come home.

* * *

Home, or at least, as far as Aldershot. The day I had been waiting for had finally arrived and I was awaiting demob. Off to Guildford to choose a suit, jacket, trousers and shoes so that once again I would look like a civilian.

Civvy street, I didn't know what it held for me but I was looking forward to it all the same

Book 2 Peace & Retribution
Part 1

Chapter 1

Peace, but I didn't feel at peace.

What had happened to Tom in Spain still played on my mind, although I now felt powerless to do anything about it. I hadn't come across Wilson again after Italy and had heard that after resigning his commission he had left for India. Still I had my own life to get on with and tomorrow I had an interview at the Reading Gas Company to resume my employment.

* * *

"Could Mr. Bristow go through to the Inspectors office, please," a request that was spoken with a disdain that showed Mr. Bells secretary thought she shouldn't have to be dealing with the likes of fitters and apprentices.

He may have been an Inspector who was responsible only to the manager who was responsible to the board, but his office was not that well appointed.

Charlie Gardner

A large rug although it may have been an off cut of carpet from the boardroom covered unpolished floorboards. The desk although large was made of unknown timber and had seen better times. The top was covered in the usual mish mash of pens, papers, and the odd trade journal, plus I could see the back of a photo frame which probably contained a picture of his wife.

"Come in and take a seat. I'm pleased to see you made it through the war safely, and I've been going through your application to rejoin the Company."

The inspector had been one of the first to voice his opinion of my cowardly action in registering as a conscientious objector in front of my work mates in the yard one morning. My offer to spread his nose over his face caused him to beat a hasty retreat to his office to the laughter of all in the yard.

"The problem is that although you were our top fitter and understood the industry, you were also one of those people that question every decision made regarding the running of the company if you didn't agree with it."

"Not every decision,' I butted in, 'only those that affected me or my colleagues. I'm not a yes man and never will be."

"Your socialist leanings were quite apparent, and caused me no end of problems with disquiet amongst the men."

He made a point of skimming through my application and previous work records before looking at me and saying, "in the circumstances I don't feel that I am able to offer you a position with the company."

His decision did not disturb me although I was a little dejected. This wasn't the first time my politics had got me in to trouble. "Still,' I thought, 'fuck 'em all, I'll survive."

Two days later whilst at home contemplating my future plans, I received a letter from the Gas Company.

Dear Mr. Bristow,

Gods Earth

I was disappointed to learn that your request to join the Company was unsuccessful.

The Chairman Mr. Browne has asked that I write this letter to ask if you would still like to rejoin the Company.

If this course of action is still to your liking then please call at my office in Gas Works Road, at your convenience, and I will make all the necessary arrangements. If I am busy could I please ask that you wait and I will see you as soon as I am free?

Yours sincerely

James Pearse
General Manager

"Where the hell did that come from?" I thought. I made up my mind to call and meet Mr. Pearse the next day.

* * *

"Where the bloody hell has Gupta got to with my drink?"

Frowning, Daphne admonished her husband, "Stuart, please don't swear. The servants will hear you and it isn't very pleasant."

"Bugger the servants and any body else that's listening. I need a drink, and I need it now. I've done nothing but listen to these bloody people whine on and on about how the bank is dragging its feet on providing finance for their tuppeny halfpenny ideas for getting rich quick," then turning to the hallway and shouting loudly, "Gupta you lazy bloody article, bring me my drink now."

A few minutes later an elderly Indian gentleman appeared with a tray containing gin, tonic and an ice bucket.

Charlie Gardner

"Hurry up man, I could die of thirst waiting for you pour a drink. If you want to keep this position you need to buck your ideas up."

Daphne taking pity on Gupta looked at him sympathetically, "You can leave that Gupta, and I'll pour our drinks. See if you can help Samina in the kitchen."

"Yes go on Gupta, run away to the kitchen before I kick your arse for you, and make sure that bitch in there knows I want dinner on time to night and it had better be edible. For Christ's sake hurry up with those drinks Daphne, I'm bloody parched."

"Your being totally obnoxious today Stuart, what the hell is wrong with you. Daddy had to pull a few strings to get you this position and you have done nothing but be resentful. We've got a lovely house, servants, and you're well paid. Why can't you settle down and make something of the chance we've got. After the problems in London you would......."

"That's right, bring that up. Every bloody time, you never let me forget if it wasn't for your father, blah, blah, bloody blah." The last words almost spat out.

"When I met you, you had a house and over six thousand pounds in the bank. Within nine months you had gambled it all away plus half of my savings. You were facing assault charges and my father; yes my father saved your skin and arranged this job. You are the most ungrateful person I know." Tears were forming in her eyes as she sobbed these last words and hurried from the room.

Wilson walked over to the tray of drinks and filled a glass with neat gin slopping it over the edges then threw in a piece of ice spilling more gin. Picking up the glass he downed the drink in one and proceeded to make another.

Within half an hour the bottle was empty, the tonic untouched and Wilson spread out on the sofa fast asleep.

Chapter 2

So the following day I travelled back to Gas Works Road and made my way to the office of James Pearse. A pleasant lady of about forty five greeted me.

"Oh, so you're John Bristow. I've been wondering what the man behind the name was like."

"Well this is the man, and what may I ask may I call you?"

"I'm Miss Snell, well Pru actually, I don't mind if you use my Christian name. I'd actually prefer it."

"Well Pru I'm here to see Mr Pearse. I received a let….."

"I know,' she interrupted. 'I typed it. He will not be long; I'm to ask if you will wait if he's busy. If you would like I can get you a cup of tea or coffee."

"I'd love a cup of coffee if it's not too much trouble."

"O.K. take a seat and I'll get you one. Milk and sugar?"

As she left the room I thought what a difference between Bells secretary and Pru Snell. She would have made anybody feel comfortable in her presence with no pretentiousness of being better than the fitters and labourers out in the yard.

Charlie Gardner

She was back in a few minutes with a most welcome cup of coffee and we sat and chatted. She was interested in the time I had spent in Spain and wanted to know why some one who had risked his life fighting for the Republicans should be a conscientious objector. I was explaining myself when a buzzer on her desk sounded and she told I could go through to Mr. Pearse's office, indicating the door to the right of her desk.

He was just inside his door waiting for me and ready to shake my hand.

"Thank you for waiting. I'm glad you accepted my invitation to reapply for your job John. I had a dread that you would ignore my letter. Please take a seat." He said this with a smile on his face immediately putting me at my ease.

I took a seat in a comfortably padded green leather upright chair. The room was tastefully decorated with a heavy striped wallpaper and wall to wall carpet, with a heavy looking rosewood desk with a high backed black leather chair. Filing cabinets and cupboards around the room matched the desk. Photographs of the works adorned the walls.

James Pearse was about fifty five years old. A shade under six feet tall, he was just beginning to show the thickening around his waist.

"Let me begin by apologising for the mistake made by Mr. Bell. When the chairman, Mr. Browne, heard of the outcome he immediately asked me to try and rectify the matter. I'm hoping that your being here will give me that opportunity."

"I must admit I was surprised to receive your letter but I am even more intrigued now that you say the chairman asked you to intervene. I didn't even realise he knew my name. Can you tell me what has happened?"

Gods Earth

A smile crossed his face, "John you have friends in high places."

Perplexed, I requested, "you need to tell me more. I don't know what you're talking about."

"Do you remember being offered a job in Palestine to run a gas works there? Well, the owner David Ben Gurrion is a friend of the chairman and wrote to him mentioning you and how you helped him and became friends. He also asked the chairman to reiterate his offer for you to become his deputy. The chairman was most impressed and asked me to find out what had become of you. He was surprised that the same day he received the letter, he found out you had been refused your old position. When you left us to fight in Spain I personally had a lot of respect for you, and I believe the chairman was also sympathetic to your wishes to leave and left instructions that you were to be reinstated when you returned."

"Bloody hell, you mean to tell me that a man I met in Tel Aviv due to the bloody war is responsible for me getting my old job back. Well God bless you David. And thank you Mr Chairman for having such a wonderful friend."

"So John, can I assume that you will be joining us?"

"It would be rude of me not to, considering all the trouble you've been to. There is just one thing however; I would like to delay my start until a week Monday."

"That's perfectly O.K. Leave it to me and I will make the arrangements. Unless you have any further questions. The chairman has told me to offer you the position of a supervisor. Your rank and letter of recommendation from the chairman's friend more than qualifies you for the position. If you accept, I think that happily concludes our business."

"Don't think me ungrateful but unless things have changed since I left, then I would have to say no at the present time to a supervisor's job. Before I was called up I was earning more than a supervisor. They receive a salary but I, on an hourly rate, made more than a hundred pounds a year more than them with my overtime. I have plans which will need money so I'm sorry but I will have to decline," I replied, rising from my chair. We shook hands and I left his office.

Walking back across the yard I saw Bell heading towards his office, "have a locker ready for me a week Monday!" The grin on my face spread from ear to ear. There was no reply.

"Right," I thought, "let's make arrangements for going to Chester."

* * *

Wilson sat in front of the two directors.

The room was quite opulent having been panelled in what he thought was rosewood. There was a picture of King George V1 on the wall together with some of past chairmen and directors. This wasn't the first time he'd been in the boardroom and he was hoping this occasion was to be a promotion. The two directors were those in charge of managerial appointments and all matters relating to staffing.

The eldest, Bhattal Choudary was the one who had welcomed Wilson to the bank and confirmed his appointment as a manager a few years back. The younger one although he must have been fifty was an Englishman, Brian Parlour. Neither looked very happy.

"Do you understand why you are here Mr. Wilson?" Parlour looked stern faced.

"Well, not really but I'm hoping it's to my advantage."

"In that case you must be more stupid than we thought. You're here man because of your conduct, not only to staff but to customers. You're here to answer these claims and

Gods Earth

save your skin if you can." Whilst Parlour spoke Choudary sat expressionless.

"I don't really know what you're talking about. As far as I am concerned I have not breached any confidences or let the bank down in any way. If I have could you please tell me what it is I have done?"

"Mr Patel, a well respected elderly gentleman in the community, was belittled and embarrassed in front of a good friend of his. Unfortunately for you that friend is well known to my fellow director, Mr. Choudary, and when he heard of your conduct wrote to me to request that you were dismissed. I have therefore called you here to answer for yourself. Have you anything to say?"

"Patel, that ignorant little shopkeeper. He comes in to my office demanding that I make an advance to enable him and this friend to purchase a factory making cotton print material for export and sale here in his shops. I told him that he was already borrowing too much and to leave my office."

Parlour shook his head, "I believe the words were "get your arse out of my office you bloody smelling wog." You then took his arm and pushed him to the door. Mr Patel and his friend, a Mr. Balasubramanyan both say you were drunk. As I could smell drink on your breath when you entered this room, I do not disbelieve them."

"Patel always looks down on me and if you check his accounts you will notice that he cannot afford to borrow any more. I may have had a drink but if you had to deal with these bloody people every day, so would you."

"Your own words condemn you Wilson. Do you not realise that we no longer run this country. The Indians have independence and it is now their country."

"Yes and look at the bloody mess they're making of it. We, the people who made this country what it is today are treated like second class citizens."

"You are an ignorant fool. You had a very good job with the bank with career prospects but with your actions you have thrown it all away. I suggest you let your father in law, Sir Daniel, know as I shall be writing to him to explain why you were sacked. Sir Daniel has always been a good friend of mine and this bank, and I would hate him to think this in any way affects that relationship."

"You've no need to fire me, I quit. I shall go back to England where I shall be appreciated."

* * *

"Well Tom I'm now back in paid employment and all things considered I'm rather pleased."

With a smile on his face Tom looked at me, "and I'm happy for you, at least now perhaps you'll get on with your life and forget about Wilson. I've accepted what has happened and I would not feel easy with you risking getting caught up in something nasty just to gain some revenge for what occurred to me."

"I hear what you say but it wasn't only you that suffered because of him. Firstly he robbed various Spaniards, secondly he robbed their churches, thirdly I'm sure he assaulted Isabella, four he leaves you to fend for yourself nearly getting you killed in the process, and finally he tried every way possible to get me a spell in the glasshouse. The man is a complete arsehole and yes I do have scores to settle with him. Anyway you needn't worry too much because he's disappeared as far as I know to India. That's enough said about him, where's Mary and the kids."

Gods Earth

"She'll be back soon. She's gone to walk the children home from school, young Will hates it as he thinks that at nearly ten he's old enough to look after himself and Susan. They've changed a lot over the last year or so, I love having them around. Bill, do you remember him, spends a lot of time with them, considering he seems to work twenty five hours a day. Mind you they do as they're told, I don't think he's ever hit them but you can tell he was in the navy; he's got a voice like a foghorn. The first time I was there when he shouted at them. He'd already told them to get ready for bed and they'd all but ignored him and continued playing. I damn nearly jumped out of my skin, when he yelled 'bed' at them It was a picture, Bill was trying so hard to apologise and the kids couldn't stop laughing at my distress."

"Only met him once and that was fleetingly. Seemed a nice bloke. What does he do now?"

"He's a builder by trade and has got himself a contract with the council to rebuild, repair or do whatever is required. Employs a couple of labourers as well. Mother has offered them a piece of land to build a small house on if they wish to make their move here permanent. The kids are settled at school here and I know mother wants Mary to stay on here as housekeeper. They get on well together and since Mary nursed me through mother trusts her completely. It's more like a friendship than an employee, employer relationship. Just as well you're staying tonight 'cos mothers arranged a dinner for all of us including Bill and Mary."

"Don't mind at all, in fact if Mary's cooking I will look forward to it. Just one thing it's not going to be too formal is it with loads of fighting irons. A spoon, knife and fork are as much as I'm used to. And I've only got my demob sports jacket and trousers."

"No, I told mother if she went too far you'd find an excuse to disappear."

Charlie Gardner

As it was the meal was an enjoyable affair. It was the first time I had spent any real time with Bill and I found him a pleasant, engaging man with a real sailor's talent for telling a tale that had been embroidered over time. Prior to the war he was a builder but whilst a boy had been a cadet sailor. Like me he had enjoyed his war service but admitted to being scared shitless many times, although he added he was more frightened for his wife and children than for himself.

After the meal the gentlemen retired to the library for brandy and cigars. Had never done this before and it felt mildly amusing to leave the women behind.

I'd developed a taste for brandy in Spain but the cognac Alan, Tom's father, poured was as smooth as silk.

What with the wine and port with the meal and now generous measures of cognac Bill's accent went from barely discernible Londoner to real cockney and he became maudlin as well.

"John I've never properly thanked you for shaving, no wait a minute, I mean saving my little girl. She's the only one I've got and I got to tell you I cried when I heard what had happened. I've got to thank you for both me and Mary. You ever want anything I can help with and you've got it. Understood?"

Chapter 3

Although life had returned to near normal, I still could not get Wilson out of my mind or the feeling of guilt regarding Tom. I knew he did not blame me one iota, and as much as I accepted this there was always that niggle in the back of my mind.

Despite all this I still managed to enjoy life and again took to refurbishing and installing gas appliances for extra cash. My philosophy that interest, rent and dividends were the bane of the working classes had not changed and I intended that in spite of the odds I would be owner of my property and although I would have to service a mortgage, I'd be damned if I would pay some idle landlord rent. These little private jobs or P J's as they were called allowed me to accumulate a tidy sum.

Work was going well and I was considered the best fitter of all those working at the company. There was still a little antagonism between myself and Oscar Bell, the Inspector.

One small incident that did cause laughter amongst the fitters and apprentices was my being chosen to fit a new cooker at the chairman's house. A couple of weeks previous to this Bell had got everybody together to inform us that

Charlie Gardner

we were taking advantage of too many tea breaks and that we should only take a ten minute break in the morning and a ten minute break in the afternoon and should refrain from accepting offers of refreshment from customers. This would be considered a disciplinary matter and wages would be deducted in lieu of time lost. Habitual offenders would be sacked.

Everybody totally ignored this missive even though Bell thought it necessary to have this typed up and placed on the notice board.

I fixed the cooker for the chairman's wife who was a really lovely and pleasant lady who asked me lots of things about my time in Spain and especially Palestine and their friend David Ben Gurrion. The job took three times as long as it should but I considered it ill mannered to hasten my departure. I was surprised two days later to be told to report to Bell's office.

"Well Bristow, explain to me what happened at the chairman's home."

Looking straight at him I relied, "Well Bell, I realise I may have taken a little longer than what was on the job sheet but I couldn't just walk away from the lady when she wanted so many questions answered, could I?"

"Don't you dare call me Bell, it's either Mr. Bell or sir, I don't care which but you do not refer to me as Bell."

"You listen to this good, I'm either Mr. Bristow or John, I don't mind which but I prefer to keep John for family and friends. In the army I was often called Bristow and I accepted it as the way of the forces, but I'm not in the bloody army now so rank means nothing to me. I have a handle to my name and anyone with the courtesy to use it deserves the same respect. I'm sure you understand."

"You are the same bolshie bastard you were before you went away. Why the hell the chairman ever let you return is

Gods Earth

beyond me. Be that as it may, what I called you in here for was regarding your visit to fix the cooker at the chairman's house. I'm not interested in how long it took to install but why you should offend Mrs. Browne by refusing coffee and biscuits."

"I did make clear to Mrs Browne that as much as I would have enjoyed the coffee and digestives, I had already had a break that morning and if I were to take another one I could be disciplined and have my wages docked. She understood but could not envisage that her husband would allow such Dickensian practices. I had to agree with her, out of courtesy of course," during this explanation Bell went redder and redder and his fists bunched tight.

"You really think your smart don't you? How you ever reached the rank of sergeant is beyond me."

"Knowing my job and having the respect of those above and below me," I said and then remembering my words to Wilson, I added, "God didn't put me on this earth to be fucked about by the likes of you."

Bell looked absolutely flabbergasted.

I continued to look at him and when no response was forthcoming, I said "Ah well if that's everything I'll get on with my days work."

On my way back in to the yard that evening, I gave way to James Pearse's car. He stopped and wound his window down, "Good evening John, I hear you had words with Mr Bell this morning. No I don't want to know what was said but I would like you to cut him a bit of slack. He has a difficult job."

"I understand and I will. Good night sir."

I noticed the next day the notices regarding breaks had been removed from the notice board.

Part 2

Chapter 4

1956

The preceding years had been busy. I was married now with a stepson, Mark, aged 21, and a boy, Charlie and a girl, Annie, of my own, twins aged 6. My wife Grace was a divorcee, much to my mother's chagrin.

The twins were at the local village school, but Mark had a job at Lloyds Bank in Reading.

Life had treated me well and after purchasing a piece of land in a village called Spencers Wood, I had over the next three or four years built a bungalow. I say I, but Bill had done the brickwork and other than feeding him and providing him with some timber he would not take any payment. When I insisted on paying him he told me I had done the plumbing and central heating for his place and he was just returning the favour. Timber and petrol were still on ration but my mothers brother owned a sawmill and let me have fuel and the timber for a very cheap price. The footings had been dug by a couple of trench diggers who worked for the gas board. Their pay was thanks to the

Gods Earth

local village butcher who let me have some black market to provide them with sustenance.

The labour was provided by my wife who toiled endlessly whilst I was at work. Even now five years later the bungalow was still not completely finished. Life was great and occasionally Tom and his wife would come and stay for long weekends.

There was a good acre of land and I found enjoyment in a large vegetable patch the results of which provided most of our requirements.

Tom had married a lovely girl called Natalie, ten years his junior and a partner in the accountancy practice. They had no children and with fifty approaching they had both decided that it would not be a wise move for them. Mary and Bill's children were now grown up but maintained a very close relationship with Tom and Natalie.

Mary had remained with Tom's parents Alan and Mary. Bill was now boss of his own building company although Will had left school at fifteen to join him and was sharing the responsibility. Will had lots of commonsense and Bill often admitted, out of Will's earshot, that he was more than capable of running the firm on his own.

I named the house 'The Pee Jaze' as I reckoned the bungalow was paid for mainly from private jobs.

It was during a weekend that Bill, Tom and Natalie were staying, that a plan was developed. It all came about from nothing.

The five of us were finishing off a few beers and gin and tonics after a fish and chip supper and putting the world to rights, when Mark returned from an evening, with friends, at The Black Boy.

"John why don't you tell Tom and Nat of your meeting with the local Home Guard when you arrived here, I'm sure they won't have heard about it."

"I'm sure they've already heard it Bill."

"Well I haven't," said Natalie, 'and from what I know of you it will have been certain to upset the local gentry."

"Oh, it's nothing really. Last year my neighbour over the road was out for stroll with this old boy who lives in that large house on the right about a hundred and fifty yards up. Well I was introduced as John Bristow the chap new to the village building a bungalow, and he was introduced to me as Major Kent. He says to me in a typical officers clipped tongue "nice to meet you Bristow, how do you like our village?" to which I replied "lovely village Kent, although some of the people are not what they seem." Well the old Major looked at me and said I prefer to be addressed as Major, so I immediately replied, "so you're still in the army then."

I took another sip of beer from my glass and continued. "He stared at me and said of course I'm damn well not man, I retired twenty years ago. Looking him in the eye I said so you're not really a Major and I don't have to salute you then. A couple of days later Dick from over the road told me that the old duffer reckoned I was a bad sort and should be watched. If he ever finds out I take The Daily Worker he'll have me shot as a subversive!"

Mark looking towards Natalie said, "Dad's always been an awkward old sod and you'll soon understand that when you've known him as long as the rest of us."

Chapter 5

Natalie smiled, "I've heard too much from Tom about John to be shocked by anything he says or does. What I'd like too know is how are you finding life in the bank, Lloyds isn't it?"

"OK, I'm just about to finish my exams. Law in relation to banking is a bit of a bugger, but I think I'll be good enough to get a pass. Most people think of banks as being stuffy and old fashioned but it's not like that at all although I did discover the other day that if I want to get married the Manager has to approve my choice of wife!"

Mark paused whilst he lit a cigarette, "They even have to approve my choice of house should I purchase one, just to make sure I don't live above my station and live in a better house than my seniors."

Bill laughed. "Just find yourself a piece of ground and we'll build you a mansion then you can tell the bank to stick its rule book up its proverbial. I'd have said arse but with Nat and your mum present I wont."

We all started laughing including Bill who hadn't realised what he had said.

"You won't need to Bill; I intend to be on my first managers' appointment within the next ten years."

"I didn't think there were any managers under the age of forty and most of them seem to be within five years of retirement. I mean most of 'em make me look young and I'm in my forties although the wife says I look to be in my fifties."

"Well my present one is in his forties although the way he drinks he probably won't see fifty. Miserable sod, usually drunk by two o'clock, and upsetting staff with his rants. We all know he fiddles expenses by claiming for things he doesn't actually do. Still he'll get his come uppance one day."

"Being a practicing accountant I would have thought the bank would have had procedures in place to eliminate petty cheating. It can't involve large amounts or it would have been noticed." Tom looked to Mark for an answer.

"Oh, it's only few pounds here and there usually but once in a while it gets to be a little larger. He's sure to get caught some day the same as one day his wife will catch him with one of his floozies. Why his wife puts up with him I'll never know, she's such a lovely lady."

For the next half hour Mark explained to Tom and Natalie how his managers little fiddle worked. Bill and I listened, but the accountant in Tom was showing interest.

Grace rose from her seat. "Anybody like a cup of coffee?"

Everyone agreed that would be a good idea and she made her way to the kitchen.

"Sounds a really nice fellow your manager. If I was his wife I'd ditch him. I'll never understand why we women stand for this behaviour; Tom wouldn't last two minutes if I caught him entertaining other women."

Gods Earth

"I often wonder why none of our female staff have never tipped her the wink. They all say that Wilson leers at them when he thinks they're not looking. Probably thinks he can get away with it here the same as he did in India."

I was concentrating on what was said previously and thought I had misheard. "What did you say his name was?"

"Wilson. Stuart Wilson he returned too England a few years back after working for the National Bank of India which used to be owned by the National Provincial Bank. Some employees stayed on after independence but returned a few years later. The rumour is that Wilson's father in law got him the position with bank. Why are you so interested?"

Tom was on the edge of his chair now and kept looking at me. "Don't tell me that bastards surfaced again. What do you think John, is it the same man?"

At that moment Grace entered the room with a tray of coffee. 'What's all the excitement?'

Nobody said anything to start with then Mark replied, "Don't know really, they've suddenly taken an interest in my boss."

Natalie and Bill started to talk at the same time. "No you first Nat. Ladies privilege."

"No Bill you probably know the story better than I do and I think its better, that's if John or Tom don't want to tell it, then it should be you."

Bill looked at myself and Tom and when we shook our heads he began to tell the story apologising that it may be necessary for either of us to correct him if he got any points wrong.

When he'd finished Mark said he couldn't believe that this was one tale that I had not related to him. However I did impress on him that under no circumstances was he to relate to Wilson that he knew of his past, and never let it be known that he was my stepson. In fact it would be better if he never mentioned me at work.

By the time Tom and I had finished answering questions it was gone midnight and they all decided to sleep on it and see what the morning would bring.

Chapter 6

The next morning Tom and Bill joined me for an early cup of tea.

"I couldn't believe what I was hearing when I heard Mark mention Wilsons name last night."

"You couldn't. I had to ask him to repeat it. After all these years I didn't think I would ever hear it again. I hardly slept at all last night. All I could keep mulling over was everything that has happened regarding that bastard. I don't know about you Tom but I have unfinished business with him."

"Look John, you don't have to do anything on my behalf. I don't know what you're thinking, but risking your life, jail or family isn't worth it."

Bill interjected, "I owe both of you so if there is anything I can do, I'm in. Don't say it's nothing to do with me but we've been friends for a good few years now so whatever I have a right."

I looked at both of them, "thanks Bill. Tom I'm not thinking of anything reckless but something that I believe they call a sting. If you don't want to be involved I understand. If you're both up for it then I'll quickly give you a brief idea of what I have in mind. No one else and that includes our wives is too know, at least for the time being. I don't even know if what I am considering is feasible. If it is workable then Wilson won't even see it coming. I don't want to ask for Marks help but it may be unavoidable."

After explaining my plan of action to Bill and Tom we broke it down in to individual plans and agreed we would go away and investigate if what each had to achieve was viable. We would also need to raise some capital between us to finance the operation. We allowed ourselves a month to begin with and would telephone each other every weekend.

Later that day I had a quiet word with Mark and impressed upon him the importance of not letting it be known at the bank who I was and my connection to Wilson. Mark promised he would never mention a word of what he had heard and I knew he wouldn't.

* * *

The following weekend I called Tom who told me it should be possible to open a couple of sole trader accounts and construct some fictitious audited accounts. We would also require a solicitor and as yet he had not yet worked out how to overcome this problem. He would continue to search for a solution to this problem.

Bill had also been busy and thought he had found the answer to our problem but that it would require a visit to his old stamping ground in Hackney. We agreed that I would go with him the next weekend. He would travel down on Friday and we would go to Hackney together on the Saturday and stay with his brother overnight on the Sunday.

Although this was only the early stages things looked promising.

Gods Earth

The next Saturday Bill and I travelled to Paddington then the tube to Holborn and then the bus. His brother had lived in Dorchester Street but it had been bombed in the war and was now a prefab village. When you considered that the war had been over for ten years you would have thought that more effort could be made to provide decent living accommodation.

Ted was an easy going fellow with a dry sense of humour. At a quick glance you could mistake him for Bill. Both had dark hair that was thinning on top and a face that always seemed to have a smile

That afternoon Bill, his brother Ted and myself set about looking for some property too purchase. Most was cheap as many streets had not yet been rebuilt following the bomb damage caused during the blitz.

One street was particularly appealing. It wasn't very long and backed on to open ground.

"Do you know who is dealing with the sale of these sites Ted?" Bill queried.

"Well a lot of these properties were part of the Hoxton estate, but as far as I know this was disposed of in the twenties or thereabouts. Other than the council there were a number of private landlords. I'll make enquiries in the week and find out for you. Tell me what the hell do you want to buy property in this area for, there are far nicer places to live in than these bomb sites."

"Maybe but I think John will agree with me that this or something similar will be most satisfactory."

I looked at Bill then Ted and said, "this would be absolutely perfect providing the price is right."

"Well, prices around here are dirt cheap even when the houses are in pristine condition. Two up two downs get about one pound ten shillings to two pounds a week in rent. They sell for about nine hundred to a grand apiece."

Charlie Gardner

Ted smiled and continued "for you affluent sorts from the sticks that will be peanuts."

Returning Ted's smile I said "absolutely right and Bill and I would like to treat you to a drink or two tonight to say thanks for your help."

"Wish I could," he moaned "but I've promised the wife we'll go and see her mother who's feeling a bit under the weather. Still you'll both be round for Sunday dinner won't you. Twelve o'clock sharp, for a quick one at the local before a full blow out."

"I'm looking forward to it. Bill tells me your Maggie could roast boot leather so that it was as tender as jelly."

Chapter 7

Later that evening Bill and I had a pie and mash supper. First time I had tried this delicacy of the East end and although I enjoyed the pie and mash the liquor must be an acquired taste that probably has to be picked up from a baby feeding on its mothers milk. Still to cleanse the palette we decided on a pint or two in a rather raucous pub.

Later walking back to our digs we discussed our next move, "Bill, I know you offered to help but if this gets a little bit dodgy and you wish to pull out, I wont hold it against you. This isn't really your fight. One thing that does concern me is the cost. I'm not made of money and although I can borrow some I doubt if it will be enough."

"It's not my fight directly,' he replied, 'but you and Tom are mates and if I can help I will. I just love the idea of it and it's because Tom and you rescued little Susie. When the war ended Tom's parents gave us a place to live and Mary a job, plus they helped me set up my building business and provided the land for me to build us a house. It's not that I feel indebted but because we're friends. I want to help. As for money I'm not doing to badly and will gladly put some money in the pot. And that's all I'm saying on the subject so please don't raise it again."

"Not bloody likely if I'm going to get a speech like that for my trouble," I laughed.

"Just tell me do you think………..Wait. Listen do you hear that? Sounds like a woman and some bloke arguing. She appears to have a problem." Bill stopped and strained to hear it again.

I heard it as well. "Seems to be coming from around the corner. Let's go."

Chapter 8

We quickened our pace not quite breaking in to a trot. We rounded the corner to see three lads goading two nuns who were probably on their way home from the local hospital. Although they could see us coming, it did not appear to bother them.

We were three or four yards away when I said quite loudly, 'right lads leave the ladies alone and be on your way.'

The only reply was from a short stocky layabout. "Fuck off and mind your own business granddad."

"I can't. Firstly these ladies are friends of mine and you're upsetting them. Secondly I'm not old enough to be your granddad and I wouldn't want a lout like you for a grandson, and third and last because I don't want to hurt you."

I noticed Bill take a step or two to put himself between the trio and the two nuns.

The tallest of the three took a step back. "What say we give these pair of interfering busybodies a little something to remember us by?" And with that he drew a flick knife from a pocket.

Charlie Gardner

Bill put his arms out and pushed the nuns towards the wall behind them and told them to get on their way. Hesitatingly they began to move away.

"The knifes mine Bill, can you give these other two a headache they wont forget in a hurry?"

"No problem mate, it'll be like spanking schoolboys."

My opponent jerked his right arm out straight in front of himself. I took a step back.

"Not so fucking brave now are you," he spat out and with his arm still out in front, lunged at me. I quickly side stepped to the right and the knife missed me by a good few inches. Taking a couple of steps back to give myself a bit more space I noticed my assailant prepare himself for another attack. Again it was straight armed and he was waving the blade by rotating his wrist. This time as he made his move I went to his left grabbed his wrist with my left hand and jabbed my elbow just below his ribcage. He dropped his weapon and sank to his knees. I let go of him and moved to pick up the knife.

I noticed movement but was to slow too avoid his kick in to the side of my ribs. "Bloody hell," I thought, "I must be getting old, I thought I'd hit him hard enough to keep him down!"

He was looking at his knife which was in the gutter when he should have been concentrating on my getting up and sending a punch towards his temple. He moved but not fast enough and my fist landed on his ear. Not deadly but very painful and he yelped out loud. He grabbed for his knife and managed to reach it. With him holding the blade again I took a step back to give myself space while he thought about his next move.

Common sense should have told him to run but anger made him steady himself for another assault. His method of attack was limited to holding the weapon in his right hand, straight armed and trying to strike my upper torso. About an inch or so taller than me he was quite slow to react. His eyes darted between the tip of his knife and me whilst I just watched the arm holding the knife. He came forward arm outstretched and a second before his blade should hit pay dirt I dropped low and his arm continued over my shoulder. My head dropped below his groin and through between his legs. Straightening up I threw him over my shoulders and heard him hit the deck knocking the wind out of him.

I turned and saw he still had managed to keep hold of the knife. Falling to my knees I snatched up his wrist and with both hands forced it back till he dropped the knife.

"Stop you bastard you're break my bloody wrist."

"Absolutely right son," I said applying quick pressure and feeling his joints give way as he screamed. "You ain't going to be holding a knife for a long time or even wiping your arse with your right hand for a while. Think yourself lucky that I'm not contemplating the other arm or your legs."

For the first time I was able to glance up and see how Bill was doing. No worries, one was on the floor and the short stocky lad had his arm held up his back with Bill threatening to dislocate his shoulder if he struggled.

Hardly able to stop laughing Bill said "Christ you army boys are slow, me and the lads here have been watching you since his first strike. None of 'em can fight which is why lanky there probably carries the knife and they only pick on defenceless women. The one on the deck went down with my first tap on his chin though this one was a bit tougher."

"Aye aye cap'n your right, I should have known, the navy stand offshore and watch from a distance! Let that poor bugger go, I don't think they'll mess with the F troop again."

Having been released the short stocky lad went over to help his lanky friend to his feet and then went over to check on his other mate.

"What's your name?" Bill asked.

Charlie Gardner

"Archie."

"Well Archie if I were you I'd find some new friends because that long streak of piss there will only get you in to trouble. Before long you'll be called up for National Service but if I were you I'd sign on now and get yourself a trade and learn how to look after yourself properly. You're not stupid so think about it. Now why don't you and your mates piss off home and try and keep out of trouble. You might want to take that one there to the casualty department and have that wrist set."

Taking his advice they made their way down the street.

Bill started laughing again, "it's over ten years since I've been involved in a ruck like that. A quiet night out for a drink with you and its like being on shore leave after six months at sea. Since when did you find religion?"

"When I was in Spain and again in the last lot I came across the sisters of mercy a few times. No I don't have any time for the church especially the Catholics and the Church of England is as they say the Tory party at prayer. Would we even have a C of E if the Pope had agreed for Henry to divorce? When he couldn't have his own way, he simply set up his own with him in charge. Hey presto divorce is no problem. Forget the populace they can be controlled by force."

"Well John I can never remember it being taught like that in school."

"Of course not Bill they teach you what they want you to believe. However what I was going to say was during the fighting in Spain food and medical help was often in short supply, but where possible if you came across a convent the nuns would often share their meagre supplies or treat wounds as best as they could. I've no doubt they did the same for the Nationalists but that was because they tried to stay true to their beliefs. The priests on the other were just as likely to betray you, not all of them, but most. As Republicans we killed some especially if they were known as Nationalist sympathisers."

"Does it not worry you or pray on your mind?" Bill intervened.

"I've never lost any sleep over it. The nuns were the same in Italy, I haven't got a lot time for the church but I've a lot of respect for the nuns. You never heard any complaints from Rome about Hitler or Mussolini did you? As you've heard me say before I wouldn't attend a church but I do believe there's a God."

"John, you never fail to astound me!"

We continued our journey in silence.

Following a really tasty lunch at Ted's, Bill and I made our way back to Paddington.

"You struggling old man?" asked Bill

"My bloody sides killing me where that bugger kicked me last night. I don't think he's broken a rib or even cracked one, but I had one hell of a bruise there this morning when I woke up. Christ knows what I'll tell Grace if she notices. It'll probably be you that takes the blame for it. Fancy taking an innocent like me to the big city and getting him drunk."

We boarded our train and although I alighted at Reading. Bill stayed on to travel up through Oxford and onward to Chester.

"I'll see you next weekend by which time Ted will hopefully have good news for us regarding a suitable property. Hopefully my ribs will have healed and Tom will have made progress with his side of things. Grace thinks you and I are sorting out Ted's heating so I'll blame the ribs on a slip!"

Chapter 9

The following weekend Bill and I met again with Ted who had found a couple of more properties for us to look at. The site that had appeared suitable the week before had become unavailable although Ted could not find out why.

We spent the day searching for other properties but with not a lot of success and at four o'clock returned to Ted's for a wash and change of clothes before going to the pub for the evening.

Following a tea of cold boiled ham with home made bread the three of us walked through the bomb ravaged streets of Shoreditch to the Red Lion public house.

The pub was fairly busy but Ted and I found a table in a corner whilst Bill got three pints in. There was a lot of noise with the usual arguments regarding the afternoons sport.

Bill returned with the drinks, "its bloody murder trying to get a drink at the bar, silly sod should get more staff. You can get the next round Ted, perhaps you'll fair better. What do you think of what we've seen today John. Anything look promising?"

"A couple of the streets we looked at seemed more than adequate for our purposes. That last one we looked at would suit us if the price is right."

"I thought so to but as you say it has to be something we can afford. I know we'll get our money back if all goes to plan but there's always the chance it could go belly up."

Ted seemed puzzled by the conversation. "I still can't figure out what you two buggers are up to. I mean who wants property in this area, its nothing but bomb damaged houses. If you've found a way to make money out of the shit that this place is then I'd like to be included."

"Sorry Ted," I replied "but you really don't want to know what we're up to. I am really grateful for your help and maybe one day you'll get to know all about it. I promise you it's not about making money although we could all do with a few bob extra. What we're about is not strictly kosher so other than your knowledge of this area, we don't want to involve you any deeper."

Ted's fingers and thumb rubbed at his chin. "Okay, I'm happy with that, but it would have been nice to have made a bit of dosh on the side. .I'll go and get another round in."

After Ted had gone to the bar Bill and I discussed if we were right to involve Ted, but Bill was adamant that if Ted knew the whole story he'd want to be a participant.

Ted returned with three more pints. Looking at Bill he said, "do you remember those blokes at the far end of the bar? Used to live a couple of streets away from us, rough lot, the old man was always in and out of clink. Whatever, they seem to be taking an interest in you two. Barman says they asked him if he knew who you were."

"Now you mention it, I do recall them," replied Bill, "shifty little bastards, couldn't be trusted an inch. Had a fight with one of them at school once. He was pinching sweets off our Jeanie, still got a twist in his nose I see. His

Charlie Gardner

old man came round to see dad but got short shrift from him as I can remember. Maybe he wants another go." Bill laughed.

That started the two brothers off reminiscing of schooldays and the pranks they had pulled, and playing truant to spend a day up the West End.

I listened and laughed along with them at some of the capers they got up.

"Right,' I said, 'one more pint then I think its time we headed back. Sit tight Bill I'll go and fetch them."

I got up went the bar and waited to be served. As I stood there I noticed someone move in behind me.

A finger prodded me in the back and a voice said, "I think you need to have a word with my boss."

Not bothering to turn around I said "if you don't take that finger out of my back, I'll snap it off and ram it up your arse."

I felt the finger push a little harder then withdraw. Still not turning I said, "if your boss wants to see me then he'd better come across to where I'm sitting and to show how grateful he is that we'll talk to him, he can save me waiting here and bring three pints with him. Tell him to make mine a light and mild. The bitter here seems to have a metallic taste."

"When I tell him what you just said, he's more likely to come across and pour your drink over you."

I looked him in the eye, "just tell him what I told you, capiche."

He made his way back and I turned and rejoined Bill and Ted.

Ted looked quizzically at me, "what happened to the drinks then? And who was that bloke you were chatting with?"

Gods Earth

"He was a messenger from your old school friends; they want to have a chat. Probably want to warn me that I'm mixing with a bad lot! I don't know what they want but I told him to tell them that if they want to talk then they can come over here and bring our drinks with them."

Ted's face fell, "great if they want a word it can only mean trouble. Ah well, we're about to find out, they're on their way over."

The brothers stood behind Ted facing myself and Bill. Both were slight figures about five feet nine inches tall and weighing no more than ten and a half stone. The one with the broken nose spoke, "I'm Nate and this is my brother Len. We hear you're interested in buying some property in this area."

I glanced up at Len then turned my head towards to Nate, "If I am, I don't see what concern it is of yours, unless of course you have property to dispose of."

Nate smiled, "no I don't have any property to sell, but I am always interested when somebody wishes to purchase on our manor. I like to look out for the ordinary man and woman who live here."

Bill stared at him or more pointedly he stared at his nose. "Still don't see what that has to with us. I might not live here but it's where I grew up."

"Maybe but you still have to pay your dues."

"So your career as school bully and petty thief has blossomed in to a collector of taxes. Let me put you straight Nate, You do not scare me and if you want me to have a go at resetting your nose then you mention paying protection monies again. My friend and I will be back again next week to decide if we wish to purchase and I suggest you make yourself scarce."

"Nice speech Bill Rose but if you look around you'll see that your outnumbered, so don't threaten me and don't come back unless you wish to do business." With that he turned and with Len in tow went back to their end of the bar.

"Thanks Bill, my ribs are still sore from last week and how am I supposed to tell Grace I'm not going to be at home next weekend! We can't fight them, although I have to be honest it doesn't matter to us what aggro they cause because we'll not be the final owners of the property."

"I know that and all you have to tell Grace is that it's taking longer than expected. You're the plumber, you'll think of something."

"Yeah and if I arrive home looking as if I've gone five rounds with Rocky Marciano she just might wonder how tough plumbing is!"

"When I started on this caper I thought it would be oh so simple. Now all I can see is problems. Last week I had my ribs kicked in, next week it looks as if I've got some east end gangster to deal with. If I wind up in hospital Bill, you can be the one to explain it to Grace."

We still hadn't had our third pint and decided that we'd call it a night.

Chapter 10

I was worried about the next weekend and had managed to contact Jack and talked it through with him, not the whole story but the provocation we were receiving in Shoreditch. Always the pragmatist his advice was walk away.

But because the purchase of cheap property was tantamount to our plan, I made my excuses to Grace and met Bill and Ted to continue with our endeavours.

We revisited the property that had interested us with a chap from the council. He told us that Ted could collect details of the council's solicitors and more factual details of the property at the municipal offices on Tuesday.

* * *

"Stuart, I'm just about at the end of my tether. I realise you no longer care for me, but when my close friends discreetly let me know that you've been seen out about with some strumpet, it's just too much." Daphne's face showed she had been crying.

"What your friends have seen is nothing but me out and about on the town with the odd customer or two. There is nothing going on and I'm shocked that you should think there is. If you're going to believe your friends over me, then there is nothing I can do, but you're mistaken." Wilson poured himself another gin and tonic. "To be honest, I'm getting fed up with these accusations you keep making."

"You don't know how much I'd like to believe you, but I've heard of your dalliances too often. I don't even feel embarrassed by what my friends tell me any more. Then there are the bills that go unpaid unless I settle them. You're either wasting the money on horses or whores. I've had enough and will divorce you if things don't improve."

"That's where you're wrong. If there is going to be a divorce it will be me divorcing you and that will only happen if I want it. Now I'd be grateful if you would carry out your wifely duties and get me a fresh white shirt, I am off to lodge this evening and won't be in till late."

Daphne started to sob again, "you want a shirt, then bloody well get it yourself." She rushed from the room and went upstairs.

* * *

Bill insisted we return to The Red Lion that evening for a drink against my wishes. On entering the pub I noticed that Nate and Len weren't there and hoped they were having night out in the West End.

Although the evening was going pleasantly enough, every time the door opened I checked to see who was coming in.

Not long after ten my evening took a downturn when the brothers with three other fellows entered the bar. They went to the other end of the bar and got some beers. Every now and then Len looked our way and smiled. My glances

Gods Earth

at the door had now become directed to the other end of the bar.

They finished their first round and Nate followed by Len got off their stools and made their way to our table.

"I'm hoping you've had time to consider our conversation last week and will be happy to meet my request for help for the poor and needy."

Bill stood. "We have and I'm sorry to disappoint you but we will have to decline the poor and needy of this parish."

"Don't make a hasty decision you'll regret. My boys have given up an evening at a party with their girls to come here. They even brought their collecting boxes with them." Nate's face hardened as he spoke. "maybe you'd like a few minutes to reconsider."

"No need, we're all agreed. Sorry Nate, you and Len will have to find some little old lady to scare. Now piss off and let me finish my drink in peace."

With that Nate raised his arm and with his finger beckoned his cohorts forward.

There was an almighty crash from the far end of the bar and we all turned to see what had occurred. One of Nate's bruisers was laid out face down on the floor and the other two were being held from behind.

It took a second look before I realised it was someone I hadn't seen in a long while. I smiled at him and raised my arm in thanks as someone at the side of me fell to the floor. At that moment Len made towards me and I instinctively shot out my arm in a punch and caught him straight in the face. He went down next to his brother, out cold.

"Christ John what the hell did you hit him with. He's got a nose to match his brothers now, and Nate's ain't looking to good again." Bill was shaking his hand to lessen the pain where he'd thumped Nate.

Charlie Gardner

I opened my hand and inside it was a roll of lead about four inches long and just over an inch in diameter. "This was to help deal with their bully boys but unfortunately Len got to feel the weight of it."

Ted was laughing, "suddenly he was coming at you and then your fist hit him and he stopped dead and fell straight to floor. It was unbelievable."

Bill reached across to another table, picked up a nearly full pint of beer and tipped it over Nate. Looking at the man whose pint he had picked he said, "Sorry about your pint mate. I'll get you another one in a minute."

"No need for that, I'd have paid serious money to watch that. No chance of a repeat is there?" the stranger replied.

I made my way to the end of the bar. "Jack you old bastard what the hell are you doing here?"

"Watching your flank, as usual. When you phoned I guessed you were having a spot of bother and persuaded Günter here we could do with a weekend in the big city. He was a POW and decided to stay on after the war and helps me on the boat now. Oh yeah, forgot to tell you, when you phoned. When the old man died, I gave up the office job and took over his boat and now fish for a living. Should I let these thugs go now?" He spoke to the two that he and Günter were holding. "You two aren't going to cause me any trouble are you?" They shook their heads. "Thought not, you'd better scoop up your buddy and go. Excuse me John but I've got to buy that bloke at the bar a drink. While we looked after these two this fellow on the floor was about to have a go at us when this chap brought his pint down on the back of his head and stopped him in his tracks. I'll join you in a minute."

I took Günter by the arm and led him towards our table, and made the introductions.

Gods Earth

When we got there Bill was stood astride and snarling words at Nate. "You ever threaten me or mine again, and the next time I put you on the floor, you won't be getting back up. Don't think of standing up. You can crawl on all fours to the door. Hopefully the locals around here will see what a total wanker you are and give you short shrift in the future."

Not wishing to antagonize Bill any further he crawled away from our table, before standing and leaving.

"Bill, Ted, meet an old friend of mine, Jack this is Bill and Ted I've told you about. I spoke with Jack earlier in the week and he decided he and Günter here could do with a weekend in London. Must say I'm pleased they did." I tilted my head and stared at Len who was still on the floor. "You try putting the squeeze on me again and you'll get far worse. You were nothing but a cowardly black marketer in the last lot whereas we all went wherever His Majesty thought fit. What I'm telling you is we formed a bond so if you want to carry on this fight let me know and I'll call on a whole fucking battalion if I have to. Now fuck off and don't let me see any of your faces anywhere near me again."

They left and we settled down to chat over old times and have a drink, which we discovered couldn't be paid for. All the regulars in that night wanted to buy us a pint!

After having said our goodbyes to Jack and Günter we staggered back to Ted's, the three of us falling asleep in the armchairs and sofa.

It was a late breakfast on the Sunday morning. Maggie was non to pleased with me and Bill, remarking that Ted had never had trouble in the pub beforehand and if retaliation was taken she would hold Bill and myself responsible.

I apologised but Bill just said that Ted was never an angel and had got him in to many scrapes in his time.

Charlie Gardner

After Maggie had left us to visit her mother I voiced my misgivings over the turn of events.

"If I thought there was going to be fights and bully boys involved in trying to set this up Bill, I would never have started on it. I'm beginning to wonder if it's worth continuing."

"I understand John and I admit I didn't expect this last little irritation and if we get more then it's probably wisest to forget the whole thing."

"Well I'm glad you agree with me because I'm going to leave it with you to let Tom know that if we encounter any more hassle then the plans off. Myself and Grace are up there in a fortnight so hopefully it will have sorted itself out."

"That's okay, leave Tom to me."

"That's what I'm afraid of. Still I must admit there's never a dull moment around you two is there. To make up for it I'll let you get me a cup of tea."

Chapter 11

The fortnight passed quickly, and I found it difficult not to keep mulling over in my mind the property Bill and I had visited, the obstacles we encountered and the plans that were still awaiting fruition.

It now very much hinged on finding the cash to purchase the property and a solicitor willing to act for us either in collaboration or blind ignorance.

At six on the Friday Grace and I were on our way to Chester. Hopefully we would be at Tom's by ten o'clock. The train was packed and even with windows open it was stifling in the compartment we were sharing with seven other people.

Two young children travelling with their parents were getting hot and bothered and beginning to annoy me. The limit of my patience was reached when they were given drinks by their mother and with their arguing and fidgeting spilt some over the floor barely missing Grace.

Raising my voice I ordered "sit their quietly and finish your drinks and don't move after that. If your mum and dad can't be bothered to control you then I will."

The father made a move to get to his feet but I just stared at him and said "don't even think about it." I reckon the look on my face told him it would not be a wise move.

Grace put a restraining hand on my arm and a couple of younger guys, probably students, gave applause. The rest of the journey continued in peace with the unruly family leaving the train at Birmingham.

Quite a lot had happened since I had last visited Tom and his parents. His father had retired through ill health and was being cared for by his wife and Mary.

In the evening Bill, Tom and I took a walk to the local pub, the Rose and Crown, and found ourselves a quiet corner.

"Bill filled me in on your weekend in the smoke and I must say with what Grace told me of your journey up on the train I'm beginning to think that maybe you're becoming a bit stressed out. You are usually so cool calm and collected."

"The spat in London was purely the fact that it was some thugs giving a couple of nuns' aggravation. The incident on the train was just two kids being a nuisance, and their parents doing absolutely nothing to stop them. If they'd been mine I would have given them a thick ear. Now forget that, let me know how you've got on."

"I gave my side of it a lot of thought. As I said the false balance sheets are no problem at all, but to find someone to complete the legal side of the property transactions is more complicated. I don't know any bent solicitors."

"Do they need to be crooked?" asked Bill.

"No idea," I replied, "I've only ever bought one piece of land in my life, but you've been buying and selling properties for years Bill."

"Hold on a sec," interjected Tom, "if we wait until tomorrow night we may find out the answer. I know you said not to tell anyone else but last weekend I was at a party and Isabella and Patrick were there. I think you and I know John, that although Isabella or her father never said anything, Wilson assaulted her. To what extent we'll never know but to my way of thinking that is more serious than what happened to either me or you."

"So how does that help?"

"Let me finish. I told her that Wilson had resurfaced but not what we were up to. She said to me that if her father ever got his hands on Wilson he'd kill him!"

"Later in the evening I approached her again and invited her and her father to dinner tomorrow evening and to stay the night. They may be able to answer any questions regarding the legal side of things for us."

* * *

"Well Rita, which one do you fancy?"

"I'm not sure Stuart, but I think Feather Duster at seven to one might be a good choice, after all my Ronnie thinks I'm at my mothers doing some cleaning for her while she's ill."

"Yes very good of your mother to fall ill this weekend. Come on lets go and put a pony on Feather Duster, there's only a minute or so before the start."

"A pony. What's a pony?"

"Twenty five pounds, have you never heard that expression before?"

Charlie Gardner

"No. That's an awful lot of money. It would take my Ronnie over two weeks to earn that."

"To you maybe, but there's plenty more where that came from. Come on hurry up or I'll never get the bet on"

Having placed the bet Wilson and his latest doxy made there way to the bar.

"Let's find a seat and have a bottle of bubbly. I could do with a sit down my feet are killing me."

"Champagne, are you sure? I've never had a bottle before, just a glass at weddings and christenings. Ooh I just know this weekend is going to be fun."

The noise at the bar dropped as the loudspeakers informed everyone that the runners were under starters' orders and then they were off and the noise increased. Feather Duster started well in a field of nine and dropped in to fourth place at the mile he was in third and at two furlongs was neck and neck for second.

Noise level in the bar was reaching a crescendo as they approached the finish.

"Come on! Come on Duster," screamed Rita jumping up and down and spilling champagne over anyone close to her.

"Careful woman, careful," from a bystander.

Twenty yards from the finish the favourite Her Joy was leading by a yard or so and Feather Duster and Red Bob were squabbling over second. Rita was still screaming and jumping up and down but Wilson had sat down at his table knowing the bet was lost as he'd placed for a win.

"We were so close Stuart. He nearly got there. I was so excited. I'm so sorry I lost all that money for you"

"The nag was miles away. I only hope you get that excited tonight. Come on lets get going before the crowds leave. It's only a short trip to Hungerford and the Bear

Hotel. We'll have an early dinner, more champers and an early night."

Chapter 12

Following a starter of a smoked fish pate, the two Mary's produced a wonderful rib of beef, with all the trimmings.

I hated formal dinners but this was a pleasant relaxed meal between friends, enjoying conversation, humour, and a copious supply of wine and beer. Alan's mother had always made sure there was beer available when I or Bill were present, knowing that neither of us had a taste for wine.

Pudding or as Mary informed me, dessert, was a whisked up lemon, pineapple, eggs and tinned milk concoction that was very light and perfect for cleansing the palate.

"Mrs F B that meal was fantastic, I've not eaten like that in a long while," I remarked, "Grace, make sure you get the recipe for that pudding, I'd sure love to try that again."

"John, don't call me Mrs F B or Mrs Fortescue – Browne or even Mrs Browne, I'm Mary and that's what you all should call me. I know it's difficult with there being two Marys' but I'm sure we're both able to know which of us you mean. And yes, I will make sure I write down the recipe for Grace."

"Well John that's put you in your place," laughed Grace.

Mary stood and asked, "do you gentleman wish to smoke while we ladies withdraw to the drawing room, or more correctly to the kitchen to clear away. I take it as read that we would all like coffee. We'll bring it through to the drawing room when ready."

Alan looked around the table, "shall we all go and find a comfortable seat and forgo formalities?"

Isabella, Grace and the two Mary's left for the kitchen carrying plates, dishes and cutlery whilst Alan, Tom, Jesus, Bill and myself adjourned to the drawing room with a bottle of cognac and a rather nice vintage port which Alan had decanted earlier. I declined a cigar but did enjoy a puff on my pipe.

"OK who'd like another little snifter before the ladies join us?" enquired Alan.

Jesus and I opted for the port along with Alan, leaving Bill and Tom to enjoy the cognac.

Earlier that evening I had discreetly enquired of Tom what developments had taken place relating to finding a solicitor to act for us. Unfortunately there was no advancement whatsoever.

Taking Tom to one side I asked, "how much does your father know of what we're up to?"

"Nothing. We said nobody else to be included and I know I've spoken with Isabella and Jesus but only to let them know Wilson had resurfaced. So long as Jesus doesn't kill him before we've had our fun I don't see a problem and I think he may prove to be useful to us. Why do you want to know about dad?"

"I didn't want to speak out of turn and drop you in it."

"You wouldn't drop me in it and to be honest I would rather he knew, but that does not include my mother, she'd probably have a fit."

"Right you've got about three seconds to change your mind 'cos I'm about to up the ante."

So saying I turned to the rest of the room and asked for their attention, "what I am going to say is going to be news to you Alan and you Jesus. Before you say anything let me finish and then I'll answer any questions you may have. The one thing I would ask is that you do not relay any of what you hear to anybody else, especially our ladies who are busy in the kitchen, God bless them."

With that I proceeded over the next ten minutes or so to relate Tom, Bill and my plan for the come-uppance of Mr Stuart Wilson.

Chapter 13

Although Alan and Jesus now knew our plan, I hadn't divulged what headway had been made, mainly because it was little, and we were struggling to make any advancement.

"So why did you not let me know earlier about Wilson. Like you I have scores to settle with this man. I have not forgotten him assaulting Isabella in Espana. For a long time I wondered if he had raped her, but she says no, although she will not tell me what happened, but for her I know it was not pleasant. I would like to be involved in this mans downfall. Anything Jesus De Molina can do to help, you can count on. I am pleased that you have found this man, but feel a little uneasy that he is living and working so close to Marlow where Isabella's and Patrick's new practice is. Still I don't suppose their paths will cross and I doubt if he even remembers her."

I rose from my seat and stepped over to Jesus and grasped him below the elbow with my right hand and clapped him on the shoulder with my left. "I'm glad to hear you say that Jesus because I'm just about to give you that chance. Whether it's possible I don't know but you probably have the answer."

"I will do anything you ask of me. I may be sixty four but I am still fit both in mind and body."

Looking thoughtful Tom mused. "You may regret those words Jesus because I am about to put a proposition to you. Don't say yes until you've had a couple of days to think it over."

With that said, Tom began, "the biggest problem to beset us is finding somebody to carry out the legal work for the purchase of a property. It's possible that with a little skulduggery on our part we could use a bona fide solicitor, but it could go wrong and that would put paid to the whole thing. Would you give some thought to acting for us in this trickery?"

Jesus puffed out his cheeks and exhaled. "I will consider your request but for a second or so only, but my answer is yes. Over the next couple of days I will deliberate the mechanics of what you wish to achieve. Listening to John relate earlier your scheme for dealing with this rogue, a few suggestions crossed my mind. The strategy seems sound but I will cast a legal eye over your proposition and give you my thoughts."

"Wonderful!" Bill exclaimed, "We are at last making progress."

"What's wonderful?" questioned Bill's wife on entering the room with a tray of cups and saucers.

Charlie Gardner

"Nothing much," I began quickly, "it's just that Mark has passed another couple of his Bankers Institute exams."

"Oh, that is good news. Please give him my congratulations John. I wonder why Grace didn't mention it." Then she returned to the kitchen to help with the coffee.

"Right gentlemen," I said, "that's the last talk of Wilson tonight. Tomorrow I suggest we all pop down the Rose and Crown to continue this away from the wives and daughter."

Breakfast on Sunday morning was late at nine thirty and was simple poached eggs on toast after the feast eaten the night before. Bill and Mary had gone home just after midnight and the rest of us were deep in the arms of Morpheus a short while later.

"Mary, because I don't very often get the opportunity I've agreed to let Jesus, John and Tom take me for a lunchtime drink. We'll be back about two thirty and have lunch then."

"Of course you can darling; I'll leave everything on the side so help yourselves. Grace, Isabella, Mary, Natalie and myself are off in to Chester for a walk and lunch at The Grosvenor! John, I'm trusting you to look after Alan, His doctor is already tearing his hair out at his lifestyle. Tom is too soft; he gives in to Alan every time. He can have everything in moderation but he does need to watch his diet. After last night I don't want him snacking on chips. If he's hungry a salad will do him fine."

"Oh well son, John, Jesus, you and I will just have to slum it and eat what we find. If you two are ready we'll go and get ready and take a slow walk round too Bill's and see if he's up for a stroll before the pub."

Fifteen minutes later we were knocking on Bills door.

Chapter 14

The five of us found a table and with a pint in front of each we made ourselves comfortable.

Jesus looked at each of us in turn, "Amigos, I have thought all night of what you have told me and decided that it can be done with little or no risk to any of us. Firstly we need to purchase the land through a solicitor and a fictitious third party, namely Bill. Once this is done I will act in the purchase of the same land for Tom and John using identities from men long deceased but using documents from Somerset House to authenticate the deception. You will use this land to obtain a loan from Wilson's branch of Lloyds Bank. By the time the fraud is discovered I shall have disappeared to America where I will take an extended holiday. I have always wished to visit the States, I have a cousin in California. You will also need an address to use where none of you are known plus of course sufficient funds to purchase the property and pay the solicitor and his fees, I shall of course charge nothing. That of course is the, how do you say, nuts and bolts of the exercise, but there are lots of pieces to be filled in."

"Bloody hell!" exclaimed Tom, "you've sorted the whole thing out in one night."

"No I haven't. That was the simple part, there's all the hard work still to be done, and we shall have to adjust our strategy as we make progress because I am sure there are things we have not yet considered."

I mused for a while, "Is it really that simple for us to avoid being connected to this if the shit should hit the fan?"

"I cannot guarantee that is so but I am quietly confident that we could all slip away from this, if the sheet hits the fan as you say. After all, if I am in America there will be nothing to connect me to you, and in any case my records will not show your names, but person's long dead. How was I, a simple Spanish lawyer to know you were pulling a sheep over my eyes?"

I laughed, "I think you mean wool over your eyes."

We all chuckled but Jesus responded "no, a simple little Spaniard would stick with the sheep," and we all laughed again.

Alan who had been sat back in his chair leaned forward and put is arms on the table, "how do you intend to finance this deal. I know none of you are poor but this will take a few thousand pounds to put in place. As Tom's father I will provide the funds needed and I won't come to any you if this goes wrong and I end up losing, after all it's only Tom's inheritance I'm risking."

Gods Earth

"Well I accept your offer Alan and to say thanks I'll go to the bar and get another round in and some sandwiches if the landlord can arrange some," said Bill.

"Before you do that Bill, I'd better point out the little flaw in this plan."

"Please John don't throw cold water on Jesus scheme." Bill looked askance.

"Don't worry Bill it's only minor and quite easily remedied. Tom and I can't act in the purchase of land from the first solicitor because we are both known to Wilson. Bill you're not known to him and could easily act with another person. All we have to do is find the second body."

Everybody went quiet and anybody looking on would see five men silent, and deep in thought.

Nobody said anything for a minute or so then Bill spoke. 'I may have a solution to this problem but I can't make any promises. I'll ask my brother Ted if he will be my partner in crime. I know this means involving another in our business so you will all have to decide if I should approach him."

"Well I will agree to Ted if you all agree. I have met him when Bill and I went to view possible sites in London. Additionally he will also have knowledge of the area and has the right accent for an east ender. Sorry Bill but you've lived here so long you've hardly have any east end twang left in your speech."

"I will back you all, and the money is there, whoever plays the part," agreed Alan.

The others quickly followed suit and it was decided Bill should go to London and see his brother. Bill said he would go on Tuesday so as not to hold things up.

"Right," I said "if all goes well we'll need another meeting to plan our next move. Jesus do you know what is involved in getting certificates from Somerset house and are you willing to do that as quickly as you can?"

"Of course it is fairly simple. I will have it done within two weeks."

Great, and I reckon by then we should know if Ted's on board. So we need to think about getting together again. I don't know about all of you but Grace is likely to think its a little odd, coming up here again in such a short while. Still I'll think of something to allay her suspicions.'

A wicked smile appeared on Alan's face, "Don't any of you say anything to your wives, I have an idea which you will hear about next week. No more to be said!"

Chapter 15

"John, we've received an invitation from Alan and Mary to attend a party for his seventy fifth birthday. Why didn't he mention it whilst we were in Chester last week? Do you think we'll be able to go? It's getting expensive all this time spent with them and we've got the twins to think of."

"Yeah, it may be difficult but I would like us to be there. I realise you haven't known them as long as me but they have always treated me so well, putting me up when I first met them and never letting me leave during the war without something that was in short supply or not even available on ration. I dare say my mother will take care of the twins for a few days. If you agree I'll pop over the road in a minute and telephone them, have you got four coppers handy?"

"There should be some in my purse, help yourself. Don't you think its time we had a telephone put in. All of our neighbours except Frank next door have one. As long as we were careful it shouldn't be too expensive."

"It's a good idea and I'll think about it." In my mind I was thinking that it was probably a necessity with what I was planning and how opportune that it should be Graces idea! I'd sort it later today as I'd heard it could take a few weeks to have installed and there had to be a number or a line or something else available.

I nipped across the road and phoned Alan to congratulate him on his idea for getting us all together again and to confirm we would be there.

Walking back in the house I shouted down the hallway. "Alan and Mary will be pleased to see us. All I've got to do now is persuade my mother to take the twins. I had thought about leaving Mark in charge but they can be such little buggers and he'll want to go out with his mates or some girl, so it's probably better for them to go to mums."

* * *

Eight days later we were on our way to Chester.

"Come in Grace and you John. Mary's in the kitchen if you want to leave your case and coat here and go through. She'll be so glad to see you. John and I will take the case upstairs and then I want to show him something in the greenhouse."

Grace slipped off her coat and disappeared towards the kitchen.

I made to pick up the case.

"Don't bother with that yet John." Alan ushered me back through the door and around the side of the house. We waved to the ladies in the kitchen as we made our way to the back garden.

I could see Tom busy with a shovel in his hand.

"I've got Tom mixing me up some potting compost; I'm too old to do that bending and shovelling now. Puts me in bed with a bad back and gasping for air if I try it."

We joined Tom. "Good to see you John. Give me a few minutes to finish off and then we'll grab a cup of tea. Natalie's down in Chester at the moment getting a few last minute items for tonight. Shouldn't be long unless she starts window shopping and then we won't see her until dark!"

Alan and I stood and watched Tom, chatting idly about everything and nothing.

"Right that's that done. Dad you've got enough there to keep you going for a year and the one after that I expect. Lets go to the house and grab a cup of tea, I'm parched."

"Thanks son but before we go back in I've something to tell the two of you."

Alan took a few steps and sat on a peat bale. "I'm arranging through my broker to sell some shares to raise ten thousand. I reckon that will be enough but there's also some spare cash in various accounts if it should be needed. As soon as it's all in place I'll transfer it to you Tom to disperse as needed."

"That is very generous of you Alan. I know I would have struggled to raise that amount of cash. Still all things being equal you should get all your money back within a few weeks, and that means if you have your money back then Wilson is up to his neck in the proverbial."

"Right, that's all sorted then. Just one thing, don't mention this to Mary or your wives for that matter."

We made our way back to the house to join Mary and Grace for a sandwich and cup of tea.

"I'll have another piece of that cake please Mary."

"No you won't Alan; you know what the doctor said." Mary pulled the plate away so John couldn't reach it.

"In the words of King George, bugger the doctor, and I know exactly how he felt."

"Alan there's no need for that kind of language and in any case he said it about Bognor not cake! John while you're with him this weekend, keep an eye on what he eats and drinks. He's got high blood pressure and gets short of breath so the doctor has given him a diet to help, not that he sticks to it."

"Nothing but salads, fish, and vegetables. Don't drink more than two glasses of wine a day or one whisky. Might as well be bloody dead, for all the pleasure left to enjoy. Mary, Natalie and Tom watching everything I do. It's bloody purgatory."

Mary smiled, "curse all you like Mr. Browne, you'll get no sympathy from me. I do however intend to loosen the shackles for your party tonight."

Chapter 16

"As far as I'm concerned you can go to hell. There'll be no more spending my money on your floozies. I want a divorce and I want it quick.' Daphne was red with anger and the words were said with vehemence"

"Darling you've got….."

"I'm not interested Stuart. I haven't got anything wrong, that's what you were going to say wasn't it? The private detective daddy hired has provided pictures, details of hotels and dates. Find yourself a solicitor and let me know the details. Don't forget this house is still in my fathers name so you will also have to find somewhere to live. Start thinking about it, I'm going out," Daphne snapped.

"If you think you're getting anything from me you're sadly mistaken. I've worked fucking hard to keep you and this house and for scant fucking thanks."

"You've provided little for either me or the house. It's my private income and trust funds that have kept you in pocket. Your present position in the bank is due to my fathers influence not your efforts. After the trouble he went to, to resolve the problems you caused in India, I would have thought you would have kept a low profile and shown daddy more respect. He warned me when I married you that you were a waster and that is why he's kept all monies and property at arms length from you.Do as I suggest Stuart and find yourself somewhere to live, this place is being sold and I'm moving to Maidenhead with daddy and mummy and will look for a house close to them."

"I'm sure if we sat down and discussed this we could work things out. Why don't we……"

"Stuart you've had the last five years to work things out and all you've done is embarrass me with a string of affairs with all and sundry. No more, I've had enough and the stigma of divorce is no longer enough for me to even wish to rescue our sham marriage. Find a solicitor; I'm going to my parents to stay."

A car could be heard pulling up outside.

"That's my taxi. If you want anything, telephone my parents, that's where I shall be."

Chapter 17

A week after Alan's party I received a letter from Bill delivered to my parents address. Until our telephone was installed I'd asked him to send anything there so as not to arouse Grace's suspicions. She had intimated a couple of times that she thought something was going on. I hated keeping our stratagem from her, but I had an inkling she would have stopped me or at least shown disapproval at the risk we were taking. The guilt I was feeling, was less by not telling her than her knowing and I going against her wishes. Likewise my father told me it was no way to conduct a marriage. If I couldn't trust my wife there was something wrong.

Bill's brother, Ted, had agreed to help us and had also found a property, or more correctly a whole street of back to backs. There were forty six in total. They were part of the Hoxton Estate originally disposed of by Lord Adlington during the last year or so of the First World War.

Terraced houses at that time fetched about two hundred and forty pounds a year rent.

Even better the whole site was on the market for seventeen thousand nine hundred and fifty pounds.

Jesus had not been in touch with him regarding a solicitor to use in the purchase and he was going to chase him up.

Three days later there was a further letter at my parents.

Jesus had come up with a solicitor in Manchester. Bill was going to arrange to see the property and then leave it up to myself and Tom to arrange an appointment

* * *

Two weeks later I arrived home from work on a Friday night to find a rather plush Jaguar parked on my drive.

As I entered the door Grace called, "John, come and see our surprise."

"I've seen it. You've brought me an early birthday present and had it parked on the drive."

A voice I recognised called back "you wish! I may allow you to drive it just once but that will be all."

"What brings you down here Bill, other than to show off your new car?"

"Oh, it's not just me I've got Mary with me as well. I needed a nice long ride to run the engine in and this is where we wound up."

I entered the drawing room to find them all sat down enjoying a cup of tea and sandwiches and cake.

Bill rose and we shook hands. I went over to Mary and we touched cheeks.

"It's wonderful to see you both, and it'll be even better if I get a cup of tea. I've had a bugger of a day."

"John you go and wash up and I'll get you a tea; I don't want you sitting in these chairs in your dirty old work clothes"

Having washed and changed Bill told me all about his new car. Three point four engine, three speed automatic and a top speed of over the ton. My face showed engrossment as did my voice but in truth cars didn't interest me one little bit.

"If all you two are going to talk about is cars why don't you go to the pub? While you're gone I can make up the bed in the spare room and Mary and I can catch up."

No further urging was needed and Bill and I got up to drive to the pub.

"Well as we're not needed here we'll just pop down to The Swan for a quick pint. Come on Bill before they change their minds. You can show me your new car."

The Swan was only a mile away in Three Mile Cross but Bill couldn't resist taking the long way. Out to Shinfield, across to Woodley then Sonning, Caversham back through Reading and along the Basingstoke Road to the pub.

For a Friday evening the bar wasn't that busy. Bill and I took a seat in the corner where we could have a little privacy.

"I popped down to bring you up to date as well as have a nice run in the Jag. Really is a lovely car. Ted has found a site that will do us just fine. A street of thirty four houses which on a back to back basis is sixty eight properties. Rent would be about two hundred pounds per annum giving an investment value of one hundred and thirty six thousand. Course that doesn't mean a lot to us as it will be sold on and in turn mortgaged. Best of all, the vendor will accept less than the asking price for a quick sale for cash. Oh! Also it's unregistered land."

"Sounds good to me. I'm not sure whether it's a little expensive for us or that I understood everything you told me but I grasped enough to realise its good news."

Bill smiled, "what it means is, you and Tom now need to get the ball rolling and purchase the property. Sorry don't mean to push you, I didn't realise I would get so excited by yours and Toms gameplan."

"I know what you mean, the more exciting it becomes the scarier it gets."

"It would be a bloody sight simpler if you had a telephone John."

"Well I've good news on that score. I could have waited months but the GPO have told me a party line has become available and I can have one next week if I agree to the shared line. Hopefully by this time next week you can phone."

Chapter 18

Everything was going swimmingly or so I thought until that new phone began to ring a week later on the Saturday morning.

"I'll get it!"

"No you wont, it's my turn."

The twins' usual response was to drop what ever they were doing and race to answer the phone.

Annie grabbed it, "double eight double three nine one, can I help you?"

Then the yell. "Dad, its uncle Tom for you."

"OK tell him I'm coming."

I took the phone. "Hi Tom, why the call?"

"Sorry to call John. Bit of bad news I'm afraid. Dad's had a stroke, not to serious but he's in hospital, mostly his left hand side. Lost the use of his arm and hand although there's still a little movement and the quacks say that they expect more to return. Hasn't affected his speech much though, gives me, mum, the odd doctor the rough side of his tongue but manages to flirt outrageously with the nurses."

"Christ Tom I'm sorry to hear about Alan. How's your mum taking it?"

"She's absolutely great, worried to begin with but once he reverted to his old cantankerous self she realised he was on the mend. What worries me is that he was providing the finance for our little scheme but at the moment I don't want to raise the matter with him, just doesn't seem right."

"Tom, forget what we're up to, Alan's far more important. Do you want me to come up?"

"No, at least not at the moment. I'll call you in a few days and give you an update and let you know about visiting. Mary, that's Bills wife, has been in to see him but I've put Bill off for the time being. He tires so easily."

"Is there anything I or Grace can do to help out?"

"Not really, Natalie's been a great help. She's dealing with everything at the office and dealing with the clients, and when she's finished there she helps mum at home. I feel bloody useless but I do what I can. I am concerned how it affects what we were up to."

"Tom, I've already said, forget it, your father is far more important. Maybe the opportunity to deal with Wilson will come again, but if it doesn't well que sera, sera."

"Thanks for that John; we will have our day with Wilson. Look I'm going to ring off now I've got a lot to sort out. Give my love to Grace, Mark, Annie and Charlie. I'll ring again soon."

"Give my love to your mum; tell her I will be thinking of her and Alan. Speak to you soon."

Putting the phone down I made my way to the kitchen to break the news to Grace.

I could see she was upset and we agreed that as soon as it was convenient for Tom, Natalie and Mary we'd visit.

Later Bill telephoned and we decided it was best just to let thing rest until we had more information. I mentioned our visiting and he said that we should stay with them so as not to put any more pressure on Mary.

Chapter 19

"Thanks Mary that was the best breakfast I've had in a long time."

"Thank you John, Bill always forgets the little compliments."

"No I don't it's just that I normally get cornflakes or porridge not a fry up including black pudding."

"Well that's because I'm thinking of you and don't want you ending up in hospital like Alan. More tea John? Mary?"

"Not for me thanks but I know John will. He drinks the stuff all day long. Well nearly, ask him to tell you about the chairman's wife one day. I couldn't stop laughing the first time I heard it, so typically John. Bloody awkward if you know what I mean."

"OK, I'll force another cuppa down and then I'll pop over to Tom's and walk some of this breakfast off. You going to come along Bill?"

"No, I'll give you an hour or two on your own then I'll walk Grace and Mary round, if that's all right with you."

Ten minutes later and I was sat in another kitchen with Mary, Tom and Natalie. The good news was that Alan was well on the way to recovery and although not perfect his functions were almost normal.

"I'm so glad you and Grace have come up to Chester. Alan will be so pleased to see you both. We'll visit him this afternoon but before then I have something to discuss with you."

"I'm intrigued, what would a blue rinse Tory wish to converse with a hard left socialist about?"

"More than you may imagine young man, and less of the blue rinse."

"All right, forget the blue rinse, but I'm still curious."

"John if you were to shut up for one moment I'd tell you!"

"You lads require money to complete a property purchase. Well having………."

"Hold on a moment. What are you talking about? Me and what lads? I don't know what you're talking about."

"John, Tom, do I look stupid. You have some hare brained scheme to deal with this chap Wilson who was the cause of Tom's problem in Spain. Before you say anything, do as I asked earlier and shut up and give me a chance to explain. I haven't been married to your father Tom, not to know when he was up to something. That last birthday party of his. He's always shunned parties unless they were for the business. It was fun watching the surreptitious ways you devised to all get together. He told me everything and don't be surprised John, but I told Grace, Natalie and Mary. You men have no idea. Any way the point is your father is not in a fit state to deal with financial matters at the moment and so the plans he'd put in place to raise some cash cannot proceed at this time. However there is a solution. I have access to our joint accounts and I have monies of my own in the building society which should be more than enough for your needs. So am I in!"

Gods Earth

I just sat there open mouthed but Tom looked at Natalie and stutteringly said, "How long have you known?"

"Since just after the party. We found it quite amusing watching you men find ways to keep in touch, and get together. Grace reckons it was the only way John would bother getting the telephone installed."

I suddenly burst out laughing, "bloody hell to think I've been fretting over keeping this secret from Grace. What I can't figure out is how she managed to keep from me the fact that she knew!"

Mary smiled, "you men are so naïve. Right, back to business. Bill will be here in a moment, so I need to know, are you agreed to me helping out in the absence of Alan?"

I glanced across at Tom then back to Mary, "I am, but I leave the final decision to Tom and Bill."

There was a knocking on the door and Natalie rose to answer it

Tom looked at me and said to Mary "thanks mum I'm more than happy to accept your offer."

Natalie ushered Mary, Grace and Bill in to the room and bade them sit at the table, then proceeded to make yet another pot of tea.

Grace winked at me, "you've sorted out these boys have you Mary?"

Bill's wife laughed, "I wish I could have seen their faces, I bet it was a picture. What a pity we didn't think to bring a camera. I hope you've agreed to accept Mary's offer."

"Subject to Bill's concurrence," I said.

"No problem as far as I'm concerned," Bill looked at me, "but we need to find another property, our first choice has been sold. I'll get in touch with Ted and find somewhere else, there's quite a few around. Tom perhaps you could let the solicitor know there'll be a bit of a delay."

Chapter 20

Daphne drove from Marlow to Reading parked in Cross Street at the side of the bank then entered by the side door that was always left open during opening hours and then straight up the stairs to the Securities department.

"Hello Mrs Wilson, can I help you?"

"Its Mark isn't it. I'd like to see Stuart if he's' free."

"He's with someone at the moment, but they must be drawing to a conclusion they've been together for over an hour. If you take a seat I'll get you a cup of tea." Mark came around from behind the counter and disappeared up some stairs. Five minutes later he returned to find the waiting area empty.

Mark let himself back in to the Security box. When he'd first joined the bank he found it an odd name and was surprised that the only people allowed in the box were Securities staff and management. There was no cash held there and yet lots of the routines were always carried out under dual control. He soon discovered that the work carried out in the box was stock and share business, Personal safe deposit, the holding of items of value in parcels or boxes, and the mortgaging of customers assets such as property, life policies, shares and cash deposits.

He walked to the connecting door between the box and Wilson's office and looked through the spy hole. Seeing Mrs Wilson he knocked on the door and entered.

"Yes Mr Smart?"

"I have a cup of tea for your wife."

"OK, put it down and tell the others I do not wish to be disturbed."

As Mark left the room Daphne looked back at her husband, "you knew I was coming, did you think that I would go away if you kept me waiting?"

"Of course I didn't. That was a potential customer. If things go well I could get a lot of business from him. Building chappie who's looking to expand in to being a landlord. Tells me he's hoping to buy in London where rental is needed and remunerative. Nice business if I can get it."

"Why here in Reading if the properties are in London? It must be easier to deal with somebody closer to home."

Wilson sighed, "he doesn't want to be to close to his business otherwise he'd be at the beck and call of all and sundry, as he said, if there's a leak or something needs repairing at the properties he doesn't want tenants to be able to be able to contact him at all hours of the day. Also there's' a partner involved and he lives in Oxford so Reading is quite handy. Anyway enough about that, what is it you want?"

"I want my divorce! You're dragging your feet and you know it. Daddy won't give in and pay you anything so you may as well give up on that idea. Your solicitor must have informed you that my monies and investments are all tied up in trusts which are water tight."

"The old skinflint never did like me. I hope his money fucking chokes him. All I wanted was what was fair. Pay me some cash, I know you've got it, and I'll sort things out. If not I could make this divorce take months if not years. I'm not going to walk away with nothing."

"My solicitor said you might say that so I've got a proposal. She has told me to offer you a thousand pounds payable on the granting of the decree nisi. That should provide you with sufficient funds to buy a reasonable house with the aid of a bank mortgage. Your mortgage will be cheap enough, the bank only charges staff two and a half per cent."

"It's not enough; I'll still have to furnish the place. I'll need three and a half to sort out this mess."

"No way. I may be able to go to fifteen hundred and you can have some pieces of furniture from the matrimonial home."

"It's not enough, I still have the car loan to clear, and solicitors' bill for this little lot. Go back to this woman and tell her two thousand or no deal."

"I'll try. I'll get back in touch with you. I must be off, I have to get back to Maidenhead."

"Just tell her two thousand or forget it. Pay up and I'll see you in court."

Daphne got up to leave, "I'll be in touch or my solicitor will."

Outside his office Daphne smiled. She'd been considering paying double what they'd settled on. She'd telephone Pat Rice, her solicitor, when she got home. At least in a few months she'd be free to take her relationship with David to the next level.

Wilson had a smirk on his face. Two grand easy money, double what she thought she could get away with. Still in the scheme of things it wasn't that much and he'd need to lay his hands on every penny he could get.

He thought back to the interview before Daphne had arrived.

The fellow was amenable enough and seemed to know about his business but was financially naïve. When he'd raised the matter of arrangement fees and valuations he'd offered him the cash to cover it there and then. I'll wait for that unexpected bonus he thought.

Chapter 21

The usual race took place for the telephone followed by a shout from Charlie that Uncle Tom was on the phone.

Having discussed the situation with his mother, they'd worked out that providing the purchase price of the property was not to excessive then his mother had enough funds available to cover the cost.

Bill had also spent the last two days in London with his brother viewing various properties. Out of five they'd looked at one was most suitable and another had possibilities. He was waiting for more details on the first property to establish whether it was registered or unregistered land. The answer would be known next week and if it was favourable he'd be making arrangements for me and Tom to visit the solicitor to put the wheels in motion.

Bill however had hit a problem which I would have to deal with later.

Jesus would be providing Tom and me with false identities to get used to for the purchase. My pseudonym was Henry Langham born in Oxford in 1917. Jesus had obtained a birth certificate from Somerset House. He didn't bother with the death certificate which showed he had died on the eighth of June 1944. Tom was to be Reginald Johns born in Crewe in 1910 and died 1914.

This was one of the points that concerned me. Could Tom and I carry through this masquerade without giving ourselves away by reverting to the norm? We'd both spoken about this and decided that we could probably restrict our appointments with the solicitor to only two or maybe three meetings and during these we would prove to be reticent in social chit chat so as to give away very little of our true selves.

Tom was more self assured than I was on this point and suggested that unlike reality I should take a back seat and shut up for a change! Amateur dramatics was one of his favourite pastimes at school.

A couple of days later I spoke on the phone with Bill.

The property is not too difficult to find, but when I sounded out Wilson for an account and possible loan I almost ran from the building. I had to go upstairs and wait for him to open his door to admit me. Whilst I was stood there I could see Mark working across the other side of the counter. How he didn't see me I have no idea. John we need to think of a way round this. Be great if he says hello Bill when I'm using the name John Salter."

"Hadn't crossed my mind that there was a chance of Mark spotting you and inadvertently blowing your cover. He's never met Ted so the problem doesn't arise. You are certain that Mark didn't see you, no he couldn't have otherwise he'd have said something to me or Grace. I know Mark is aware of the story concerning Wilson but I really do want to keep him out of it."

"No don't worry I'm sure he never saw me, but it was a close run thing. Have to be careful next time I see Wilson. I was thinking that perhaps Ted would meet him next but only to drive him to the French Horn at Sonning to meet me for lunch. I've always fancied stopping there for a bite to eat, ever since you showed me the place. From what Mark says he always on the lookout for anything that costs him nothing so the French Horn should appeal."

"Pity I can't meet you there I'd like a lunch at the French Horn. It sounds a good plan and at least this way you can avoid Mark spotting you in the bank."

"I'll work on it. Now, about the property, Ted found a slightly smaller development but I think it'll meet our requirements. Still haven't found out if it's unregistered but that should be through in a couple of days. It's awkward because we can't give the agent an address so we have to telephone every couple of days. We need an address for us to use that wont lead back to us."

"It's all these little niggling things that pop up that cause delays. I'd love to get this over and done with now that we've embarked on this. I reckon we could look at a PO Box number. I'll get in touch with the post office and find out what's required."

We talked for a while longer mostly about family and work and of course Bill brought me up to date with his Jaguar.

"Look Bill I'm going to have to go in a moment, the twins want a hand with their homework. As soon as you know about the property give me a bell and I'll arrange with Tom to visit the solicitors. Hopefully we'll proceed with nothing else going wrong."

Ringing off I went to prepare for an evening of comprehension tests!

Chapter 22

It was nearly two weeks before Tom and I had a meeting with the solicitor regarding the purchase.

We couldn't figure out where Jesus had found this man but he was just what we wanted. Although it was only ten o'clock in the morning he reeked of whiskey and kept mixing Tom and my aliases. His suit matched his dishevelled look. The office wasn't actually in Manchester but away from the centre in some street that had suffered bomb damage in the war and looked as if it was ready for demolition. His brass plaque "Richard White and Associates" was filthy with dirt and ver'digris.

His desk was covered in files and correspondence and my only doubt was whether he would actually be able to complete the purchase and if he did would we ever find the deeds again once they entered his office. He saw my gazing at the mess and quickly remarked that his secretary was away for a few days with sickness and once she returned all would be restored to order.

To give him his due he made copious notes and said he would contact the council's agent within the next day or so. He agreed that the documents would be ready within the month after contracts were exchanged and we could call and sign the transfer of title soon after. Thanking Mr White for his time and seeing us at such short notice we left his office.

"Blimey!" exclaimed Tom when we were back on the street, "I don't believe that was a solicitor's office. Didn't happen to see any proof he'd obtained his articles did you?"

"Christ knows what property we'll end up with but I wouldn't be surprised if it's not the one we're expecting. I wanted to correct him every time he mixed our names up but thought the more confused he was the better for us. Come on Reg, let's go find a coffee house."

"Fair enough Henry or do you prefer Harry," said Tom laughing as we made our way to the city centre.

Having walked back to the city centre and not finding a coffee house that we fancied we entered a Lewis' department store and made our way to their cafeteria.

"I have to tell you Tom but I feel as if I'm shaking. This may be what I've wanted in a long time but now it's here I can't say that I'm not worried. Not for me but for you and Grace and the kids and everybody else that's involved."

"John we've all gone in to this with our eyes wide open, nobody will blame you if it goes wrong. Plus we've gone over the plan loads of times and any risk is minimal. And don't forget, I to have my reasons as does Jesus. The only two with no axe to grind other than they're our friends is Bill and Ted. In their case I think with Bill he's trying to repay a debt for our saving Susie, even though we've told him there is no debt, For Ted, it's the thrill of being involved. Look, a few months down the line and we'll all be laughing at the way we've pulled this off. If nothing else happens at least after this we'll be the owners of some prime real estate in Shoreditch!"

I gave a nervous laugh, "we could always get Bill to develop it for us and then I could despise myself for being a capitalist landowner and landlord."

"Please don't join the bourgeois, my mother would lose her claim to fame at the local conservative party and Women's Institute, that she is friends with a red under the bed. And keep this to yourself but one of her friends told Natalie that she said if she was younger she'd have him on top of the bed!"

"Bloody hell I'd better make sure that I don't get left in a room on my own with her, mind you she's still a very attractive lady."

"Hey, that's my mother you're lusting after. From now on I'm going to chaperone the pair of you!"

The banter carried on in the same tone until we finished our coffee and cakes and left for the railway station. Tom to return to Chester, and me to Reading.

Chapter 23

The following day I phoned Jesus to let him know that the purchase of Hyde Road was underway. I had one question for him and that was what do we do with the monies from the bank loan?

"Yes, I can see that is a bit of a problem. Firstly you need to repay Mary for the capital she put up. Then I would open an account and call it Hyde Road. If Tom's agreeable I suggest you open it at any bank except Lloyds in Manchester. Ask White to introduce you to the bank and make any necessary arrangements and provide a reference if they require one. For any other information tell them to call upon White the solicitor." Jesus told me that he would think things over and contact me in a couple of days.

It was four days later that Jesus called me.

"John, I've already spoken with Tom and explained to him what I'm going to tell you. In a few days you're going to see Richard White again to sign the documents for Hyde Road. Ask him if he is able to open an account at Lloyds in the name of Hyde Road on which you will be the sole signatory. I know I initially said not Lloyds but having thought it through I don't think there's any great risk involved and for the final outcome I think it will make the conclusion easier. You will call at the bank later to provide specimen signatures and anything else they require. Ask for an open cheque book so that you can make cash payments, we cannot risk cheques being paid in to an account that may assist tracing any one of us. The only amounts to be withdrawn are for reimbursement of fees and costs, and repayment of Mary. All of this to be done on a cash basis. This will leave a quite substantial amount sitting on the account which can be left until the balloon goes up. The reason I want you to deal with the bank account is that Tom's slight limp and the damage to his ear could have repercussions. Does that make sense to you John?"

"Clear as daylight. Where as I never notice Tom's limp or misshapen ear to somebody else it probably sticks out like a sore thumb."

"OK once the exchange of contracts are signed we will leave it a week then you can tell White that you received an offer for Hyde Road and the purchaser's solicitor will be in contact with you. Instruct him to forward the unregistered deeds to the new solicitor who will deal with the registration at Her Majesties Land Registry. Make sure he understands he will be paid in full. From what I've heard White will jump at the chance to be paid for doing nothing. When I receive the deeds I will attend to the rest. This may take a few weeks or should I say months, as first registration is investigated. Also the council will not release deeds to White until completion and they have received their monies."

"Well I think I've got the gist of that but other than giving White fresh instructions there's not a lot for me to worry about. Just tell me one thing how did you find a cretin like White. I doubt if there's a minute of the day when he's sober."

Charlie Gardner

"It was actually Patrick that put me on to him. He'd dealt with him a year or so back and wound up going to Whites office to sort out some paperwork. It appears White lost his two sons during the war and has struggled with life ever since. Professionally he's okay but he anaesthetizes his personal life with drink. He won't let you down."

* * *

Wilson drummed his fingers on the desk. Damn man had a cheek telephoning him at his office to ask when he would receive payment of his account.

"As I told you a couple of weeks ago I'm at present going through a divorce and when it's all settled I'll pay your damned bill. It's only a couple of fucking hundred quid. It won't hurt you to wait."

"No Stuart it won't but I'm not going to wait forever. I didn't get my money by allowing people to get away with what they owe me. When will this divorce be settled?"

"Within four months I hope, I want to see my money as much as you want to see yours. I'll be in touch." Wilson put the phone down before Ray Over his bookie could say any more.

Wilson closed his eyes and leaned back in his chair. He needed to get some monies from somewhere. Over wasn't the only one he owed.

* * *

Nearly two weeks after our first meeting I telephoned Richard White who informed me he was now ready to exchange contracts and would require our signatures to the documents and ten percent of the purchase price as a deposit.

He didn't think it at all strange that we asked him not to use the addresses we had provided for the documents as our wives were under no circumstances to know of this purchase. The addresses we had provided were the last known addresses for our aliases and we didn't want to risk post being returned to his office.

We asked him for a week to sort it out to which he said that would not be a problem.

After ringing off I spoke with Tom and following that I dialled Bill's number, got Mary and asked her to get him to call me back.

Later that day Bill returned my call.

I explained that the purchase of Hyde Road was now ready for exchange of contracts and that White the solicitor was asking for signatures to the contract and a ten per cent deposit. He agreed that he and Ted would arrange to see Wilson and get the account open and the opening gambit in the request for a loan underway.

Three days later I met Tom in Manchester. He'd brought with him the deposit in cash plus two thousand extra that was to go in the account at Lloyds That White had arranged to be opened for us. Tom waited outside the bank while I went in and signed the bank documents.

"Well that should be the last visit we have to make to Manchester, in a few days time we can ask White to transfer all the paperwork to Jesus."

"Yes Henry, I'm going to miss our little meetings."

* * *

Ted entered the bank through its Broad Street entrance and walked to the far end of the banking hall and stood behind two others at the enquiries desk. When his turn came he explained he had an appointment with the manager and was directed up the stairs to a small waiting area.

Whilst he was waiting he heard a voice, "is that you Bill?"

Gulping Ted turned and replied "No, I'm Joe Bright and I have an appointment with Mr. Wilson."

"Sorry but I mistook you for a friend of my father. You're the spitting image of him, well maybe not exactly but very close. My names Mark I'll let Mr. Wilson know you are here."

So saying Mark turned away and slipped back in to the office.

Ted wasn't sure whether to burst out laughing or run from the building. "Fucking hell," he thought "I nearly said no I'm Ted, Bill's my brother."

His thoughts were interrupted by Wilson appearing at his door and asking Ted to step inside.

"I'm very pleased to meet you Mr. Bright. Your brother explained that you would call to introduce yourself and we should then pop along to join him at the French Horn for luncheon. It's a very fine restaurant."

Having asked Ted to take a seat, Wilson asked if there was any thing he wished to discuss before they left.

Ted asked if he could open a cheque book account in the names of Salter and Bright. He had eleven thousand to deposit some of which was in cash and the rest to come from the solicitor once the account was opened.

Wilson produced an application form and signature cards which he proceeded to complete asking for details such as full names and addresses. Again last known details for their nom de guerre were used together with the excuse that under no circumstances were items to be mailed as Joe was having marriage difficulties and if his wife found out she'd make his life hell. If John's address was used and his wife found out she would be straight on the telephone to Joe's wife and the result would be the same. He would spend the rest of his life as a eunuch.

Wilson laughed and said he fully understood as he was going through a divorce and his wife was trying to take him for every penny she could. 'I've worked myself till I'm fit to drop to keep up with her spendthrift ways and stayed a loyal and faithful husband, but it was all in vain. She appreciated nothing."

"That's just what I'm trying to avoid," replied Ted.

"Well if you sign these forms and give me a couple of specimen signatures, I'll get John to sign them at the restaurant."

Having to sign as Joseph Bright for the first time was a little disconcerting but Wilson attention was elsewhere and didn't seem to notice Ted's trepidation.

Wilson rang someone in another part of the office and asked them to bring him a cheque book and paying in book for a new account Salter and Bright.

"Can I pay in this four thousand five hundred that I have before it burns a whole in my pocket?"

"Yes my clerk can take it to the cashier and we will collect the receipted paying in book on the way out."

* * *

The drive out of Reading along the A4 to Shepherds Hill, and then left and on in to Sonning village, was uneventful with the conversation more idle chit chat than meaningful exchange. They crossed the narrow bridge and pulled in to the car park.

"That's John's car over there so he must be inside already, probably enjoying a pint."

"Nice car, wouldn't mind having a spin in that myself," said Wilson walking over to the Jaguar and peering through the windows.

They entered the reception area and crossed to the door to the restaurant. The Maître de made his way towards them.

"There's John over there by the French windows overlooking the river, and just as I suspected with a pint in his hand." Ted indicated to the Maitre de where their companion was seated.

Wilson and Ted joined Bill and chatted about the beautiful view of the river and countryside. The waiter brought them menus and informed them of the chef's specials. All three ordered the minestrone soup as a starter with Wilson and Ted ordering the steak and Bill opting for the special of steak and kidney pudding. Wilson chose a wine which Bill spotted was far from the cheapest on the wine list. Bill stuck with his beer which he said was far more suitable with the steak pudding.

The soup was served quickly and Bill decided to move the business on, "I've already outlined our proposals for the purchase of a holding in London, the properties of which would be let. Joe and I are hoping that the bank would lend sixty five per cent of the purchase price, with us providing the remainder plus the costs. The street we're looking at has forty terraced properties let at two pound ten shillings per week which on an investment basis over ten years values the street at fifty two thousand pounds. We have to pay fifty five thousand as the seller wants a premium and since this governments new rent act, then the rents are going to rise. They're almost double what they were two years ago and I think by the end of this year they'll be three pound a week."

Gods Earth

Wilson stroked his chin, "your reasoning is sound and you appear to know what you're talking about. At least you didn't tell me each house was worth seventeen hundred pounds valuing the site at sixty eight thousand."

"No," replied Bill, "I understand you bankers only value rental properties at ten times annual rental income. Not that it matters to Joe and myself, we've got enough money to cover the rest."

Wilson sat back in his chair, "OK in principle I agree to your request subject to one or two little formalities that will have to be observed." He stopped talking while the waiter appeared and removed the soup dishes.

Whilst we waited for the steaks and pudding to arrive he resumed, "Unfortunately I can only agree loans up to three thousand pounds so I will have to submit an application to my head office for approval. I will recommend the loan and I don't see any problem with their sanction. I will suggest interest of three and a half per cent over the bank rate and an arrangement fee of one and a half per cent. I know you want sixty five per cent of value but bank policy is fifty per cent. We'll match you pound for pound. I will ask for thirty thousand but am unlikely to get it. As requested I'll ask for a term of seven years. The bank will require a first mortgage of the property with the documents to be signed in front of a solicitor. You will have to bear his costs and the registration fee. There will also be a valuation fee which the bank will pay and then ask you to reimburse. I think that's about it, do you have any questions."

Because Bill had more experience of banks through his business dealings, him and Ted had agreed beforehand he would do any discussing of terms etc.

"I was hoping to closer to two and a half over bank rate and only one per cent for the arrangement fee, after all you're more than adequately secured."

"Well I'll see what I can do but would have to go along with whatever my advances department sanction, I will try though," spoke Wilson who was already considering how much of this he could turn to his advantage.

"We need to go ahead with this next week so what will the time limit be? Will funds be available?"

"I cannot allow any drawdown until I have sanction from my head office and an undertaking to register the banks charge contemporaneously with the purchase. As its Friday to day, I will get the application off by Tuesday at the latest and hope to have a reply by next Friday. Will this cause any problems?"

Playing down his knowledge of how banks worked Bill replied, "I was hoping to pay the solicitor Wednesday but not to worry Joe and I have already checked with our mother that if the loan was turned down she would let us have the money until we could arrange finance."

"I'm not turning you down it's just that the amount is far in excess of what I can agree which means I must get head office approval. I am confident that this will be forthcoming. You won't miss out on the purchase, will you?"

Ted replied "probably not as we have already covered this type of situation with our mother. Still if that's the procedure we'll just have to wait. Not to worry lets enjoy our meal I can see the waiter heading our way."

Following the main course they all chosethe bread and butter pudding for dessert.

Ted settled the bill and the three of them said their farewells in the car park.

"I'll get my solicitor to contact you so that you can send him any paperwork that you require."

"Thanks John, it's been a pleasure meeting you and Joe. When the dust settles, we'll get together again. By the way

Gods Earth

get your solicitor to forward me a copy of the Land Certificate for my records. It'll help me get things underway."

"We will Stuart, we'll look forward to it."

Bill and Ted climbed in to the Jag and Bill gave it a little bit of throttle to kick up the gravel as he pulled away.

"Arseholes," thought Wilson as they drove off towards Caversham, "still they have money and are naïve enough for me to have a bit of it." He climbed in to his car and thought bugger the office, I'll go home and call it a day.

Chapter 24

As soon as Bill and Ted made Chester they headed for Tom's house to bring him up to date with their afternoon. Although it was late evening they knew Mary and Alan together with Tom and Natalie would still be up.

"He's gone for it hook, line and sinker. You could see the pound signs in his eyes. We didn't push him to hard and led him to believe that the family had money if push came to shove. Ted played a blinder and I'll let him tell you of his encounter with young Mark."

Bill stopped for breath and another sip of his tea whilst Ted related his yarn involving Mark.

"So far, so good. If you don't mind Bill I'll phone John in the morning and bring him up to date. We'll have to contact the solicitor next week and explain that we've sold the property on and that the new purchaser's solicitor will take over. John was going to visit him regarding the opening of the account and too thank him for his help and so that he had all the details for Jesus."

"No that's OK Tom, I've got more than enough to do tomorrow. I'm going to run Ted back to the smoke and Mary's coming with us and I've promised her a night out with some of the friends we left behind when we came up here. It's been three or four years since we last went down together, although of course I've been down with John. With a bit of luck we won't run in to Nate and Len!"

"Well that's for tomorrow," interjected Ted, "how are you feeling Alan, I heard about your stroke of bad luck and all I get from Bill is "the old boys as strong as an ox, all its done is make him more cantankerous," how are you really feeling, you look great?"

"More cantankerous!" boomed Alan, "cheeky sod. This has taught me to mellow a little, I've been lucky. I could have ended up like an old colleague of mine, unable to look after himself any more and unable to talk. No way am I getting crotchety in my dotage."

"For a man who's never laid a brick or mixed sand and cement you have enough to say and tell me how I should be running my business when you come nosing around in my office. I know the real reason your there is to see if I will offer you a drop of my whiskey and you get bloody narkey when I don't. Admit it, the only one you have any time for these days is young Susie."

"That's because I'm seventy six in a month or so and she's the only one that lets me enjoy the things in life that bring me pleasure without making me feel guilty. If I was fifty years younger, if only."

"Well I wouldn't want you for a son in law," guffawed Bill and we all started laughing.

With that Bill and Ted left.

* * *

Tom spoke with John in the morning. They both laughed at Teds chance meeting with Mark.

"Wilson was the last character needed for this little charade to play out, lets hope all goes smoothly and we've given him enough rope to hang himself. It will never be sufficient to repay what he did to you Tom, but at least he won't get off scot free. Meant to tell you I had a little win on the pools last week, it won't be a life changing amount but it was a first divi plus some minor ones. There were thirteen draws but it may be a few hundred. I've not told Grace but once this is settled I may follow Jesus to the States and go and see Gary in Oklahoma. We still keep in touch and he keeps asking me to visit. If there's not enough for that I'll take her to Italy."

"Lucky you. Not considered Spain though?"

"Bollocks to Spain. As much as I liked the people we met, I wouldn't go while that bastard Franco's in power."

"Well it isn't over yet not until we've purchased Hyde Road and Wilson's lent the money."

On the Tuesday Tom and I forwarded a letter Jesus had prepared to Richard White asking him to send all paperwork to Jesus. A cheque for his agreed fee plus a bonus of one hundred guineas to compensate the loss of business was enclosed and seemed to work the trick, because three days later Jesus telephoned to say he had the documents and would go ahead and register the land as soon as the balance was paid to the council. He warned us that this would take a few weeks and not to worry if things appeared to be at a standstill.

As it was it took nearly three months before Jesus told us he had registered the banks charge and forwarded the charge certificate to the bank together with a statement that John Salter and Joseph Bright had a good and marketable title to the property.

Bill telephoned the bank and asked if they were able to open the loan and forward the proceeds to Jesus. Although they had managed to get thirty thousand they had to pay three and a half per cent over the bank rate and a one and a half per cent arrangement fee.

The clerk explained although everything was in order, the manager would have to agree the loan being opened and the monies released to our solicitor. Bill said he would be in Reading and would pop in at eleven thirty the next day. After checking with his manager he informed Bill that would be fine.

Wilson agreed to take one and a quarter per cent if it was paid in cash. He also mentioned that a friend would do the valuation for the bank and he would also like cash. Bill nipped downstairs to the cashiers and withdrew four hundred and fifty pounds which included seventy five pounds for the valuer.

"It's been a pleasure doing business with you John, and I'll get the loan opened and a bank draft on its way to your solicitor tomorrow. Give my regards to Joe and should the two of you find more projects where assistance is needed then I would be pleased to help."

It was now fingers crossed time.

Chapter 25

After the draft had cleared through Jesus' account he paid sufficient in to the Reading account to cover six months repayments, then paid the rest as cash to Mary and the account in Manchester.

Two weeks later we all got together in Chester to celebrate. Grace and I arrived on the Friday night and after rising late on the Saturday morning Bill and Mary joined us all for a late breakfast which went on for two hours.

"I hope you've all had an abundance because I would suggest that none of you eat anything further until tonight because it's not going to be here, as I and Alan fibbed when we said we would provide dinner tonight. I've decided I've had enough of cooking today." Mary then stayed silent.

"Well come on then Mum," voiced Tom, "what are we doing tonight?"

"Don't worry," said Alan, "your mother and I will make sure you don't go hungry."

Probably the most auspicious hotel in Chester is the Grosvenor and Alan and Mary had booked a table for twelve of us.

Gods Earth

That evening the bunch of us feasted on a sumptuous five courses followed by liqueurs and brandy. The usual crowd had been joined by Ted and Maggie, and Jesus and Isabella.

At the end of the meal Alan rose, "I'm not going to say a lot, but I have to mark this occasion with a short speech. Mary and I have to say a heartfelt thanks to all of you. From the letter from John and his subsequent visit to let us know of Tom's death to further trips he made to see Tom and boost his spirits. And of course Mary who together with her children nursed Tom back to full health. I feel jealous that I never enjoyed the type of friendship that exists between all of you. Like you, I cannot wait to see the outcome for Wilson. Mary and I thank you from the bottom of our hearts and are so pleased that we were able to help in some small way.' At this point Mary moved to stand at Alan's side. 'Please all of you remain seated whilst Mary and I raise our glasses to you all."

Glasses were raised and a toast drunk, followed by others as the evening progressed. Eventually it took three taxis to ferry us back to Mannings Lane

* * *

It was nine months before fruition was reached. Jesus was in America having passed his practice including the papers on the Wilson caper to the new practice. Any documents that would have incriminated any of us were unfortunately missing.

It began with Mark arriving home late from work one evening.

"Of all the bloody luck there it was a quarter past three when the front door bell rang. At least the young lad who answered it had the sense not to admit them but to ask them for identification."

"Very good of him Mark, but who are 'they' for god's sake?"

"Sorry dad, I thought I'd said, the bloody inspectors arrived today. Course all hell was let loose. The sub manager warned everybody so that all cash and valuables were either locked away or under dual control and the keyholders actually had possession of their set of keys. I've got the bottom set for the securities safe and bearer cupboards. Probably means working late every night for the next couple of months. They go through everything since the last inspection with a fine tooth comb looking for mistakes, ignored rules etc. It also means we have to be extra careful not to make any cock ups while they're around."

"You can't mean everything. How many years work is that? How many is there, seven, eight? Forty peoples work, it would take them years."

"No they go through our procedures, ensure we don't compromise keys, that rules have been observed or adhered to, check cash and all items such as parcels, share certificates are actually there or we have a receipt for there release. They check our lending is correct and being repaid as agreed and that any security is in order and could be relied upon if the bank needed to sell it. It causes chaos the things they turn up to be rectified and they don't give you a moment's peace until it is."

"Well," I thought to myself, "is this where Wilson gets his come uppance?"

The next day I telephoned Tom and gave him the news, "of course it doesn't mean they will spot anything but the loan is now three months in arrears and he has no contact with the account holders. According to Mark

Gods Earth

these inspectors check everything so they must discover something is wrong."

As it was nothing appeared to happen regarding the loan leaving us all disappointed.

Chapter 26

The inspection of the bank records was completed after four months and although we were all disheartened we commiserated that we had done our best and although we had failed it had cost nothing. Little did we know.

Mark arrived home one evening looking tired.

"You all right son, you look absolutely knackered?"

"I'm just worn out. I've had a bloody awful day. It's taken me all bloody week to prepare a report for our realizations department. There's very little information on the customers PMC and I can't trace either of them. Can't even get hold of the solicitor involved. The person now responsible for his old clients says the papers are in a mess but he will come back to me as soon as he finds them. There's twenty eight and a half thousand outstanding on the loan and the servicing account is well overdrawn. And Wilson expects me to find the answers. One of these days I'll say bollocks to the job and punch the obnoxious little bastard on the nose."

"Whoa there son, you don't want to do anything rash. He'll get his one day."

"Fuck me gently,' I thought, 'I never expected this to land in Marks lap."

"Don't worry I wont do anything like that. None of it can be laid at my door."

"Nobody like that is worth losing your job over. You've done well since you've been there and you said the inspector gave you a good report."

"Your right I'll get changed and then go up the pub for a drink. Come along if you like, I'll stand you a pint old man."

"Cheeky bugger for that you can buy me two. I'll just tell your mother."

Keeping my thoughts to myself I made a mental note not to probe Mark for information in case he became suspicious.

The next day I let Tom know that with luck, the shit had hit the fan.

Then, as before. everything went quiet.

After a few weeks I raised the subject with Mark.

"Job going better now, since that report you told me was giving you gyp."

"Yeah, works OK. What report was I going on about, the one I got from the inspector?"

"No, something about a loan, where you couldn't find the owners, or much else."

"Oh that. The accounts are in realizations now so it's up to head office to sort out now. Why are you asking?"

"Just that you were down at the time and I was thinking what happens when people fail to repay their loans. Main thing is that you're OK."

"As I said it's out of the branchs' hands now. Head office will decide how to proceed. If they can't trace the account holders then they will go for power of sale and sell it to repay the loan and current account. Could take months the speed they work at."

"So the bank gets its money back whatever happens?"

"Yes, the property was worth double what was lent. By the time the solicitors have had their fees out of the proceeds the remainder will sit on an account until someone claims it."

"Ah well, alls well that ends well."

"Anything else I can tell you. Shall I ask if there's a position for somebody to chase bad debts?"

"You cheeky sod, I was only taking an interest."

Chapter 27

"Dad last week you were asking about that bad debt I had to report. Well all hell has been let loose. Are you listening or are you reading your horoscope?"

"Sorry Mark I was just finishing off this article in the *Express* about the gas industry. Go on I'm listening."

"I told you the bank would sell the property to get its money back. They can't, well they can but its not worth the valuation of fifty thousand that Wilson put on it. I remember writing out the waiver of a professional valuation where he put a conservative value on a forced sale basis. The inspectors came back yesterday and are turning everything upside down looking for any more properties he's valued and where the bank could now be at risk. Wilson is suspended pending the outcome of an investigation. The more senior staff reckon he's had his chips. The valuers' reckon it's not worth much above five thousand although I remember they paid fifty five thousand for it."

"Well in that case how does the bank reckon its worth so little?"

"Simple it was fraud and because of Wilson's shortcomings it was easy to carry out. When the solicitor forwarded the charge certificate to the bank the manager inspects it to ensure all is above board. Sure enough it gave Salter and Bright as owners and stated that the land was freehold with absolute title and the banks charge was shown in the charges register. Sometimes if title to the land is not strong it could say good, or leasehold or even possessory. What has happened caught Wilson up to his usual tricks. In the ownership section it shows in the end column the consideration paid. This was written as fifty five thousand pounds. Wilson knocked five thousand off and valued it at fifty thousand. The solicitor may or may not have known when he registered the details, the true value."

"Fair enough. But why such a big difference?"

"Wilson claimed expenses for viewing the property but never bothered. The bank has since discovered it's a bomb site from the last war still awaiting clearance and redevelopment."

I couldn't help but chuckle. Wilson fiddles a few quid in expenses and costs the bank thirty thousand quid.

I don't think Mark noticed but I could hardly contain my joy at what I was hearing. At last Wilson was repaying the debts he owed to all those he had robbed, swindled or wronged.

I was glad not just for them and for me but especially for Isabella, Tom and Jesus.

After informing Alan of our success we decided I and Grace would travel to Chester the next weekend and we'd all celebrate except Jesus who was still in America.

Epilogue

The knocking on the door woke him, "Bollocks it must be the blokes to fix the heater."

Just his luck that yesterday when he went to have a bath there was no hot water. That was one of the problems with a bedsit and having to share the bathroom and kitchen.

He shouted out of his upstairs window, "give me a couple of minutes, I'm upstairs."

He trudged slowly down the stairs and opened the front door.

"Hi, I'm Ken. Me and my mate are here to fix the water heater. Can you show me where it is?"

"Certainly, where's your mate as you put it?"

"He'll be here in a minute, he's bringing the tools. Show me where the heater is and I'll let him in when he knocks."

"Good 'cos I've got enough to do without running up and down these stairs to let workmen in and out."

He turned, "follow me I'll show you the bathroom. It's at the back. Don't make any noise or mess and make sure you clean up behind yourselves. I've plenty to do without cleaning your bloody mess up."

Having shown Ken the bathroom he disappeared up the stairs.

It only took just over an hour to fix the heater.

"You take the tools back Ken, I'll see if matey boy wants to check that it's working before we go."

"OK see you in five." Turning Ken picked up the tools and discarded parts. On passing the foot of the stairway he shouted up that the heater was ready for inspection.

"Bloody hell what do they want now, can't they just finish the job and go. Fucking work men I suppose they want a tip. Well they can bloody well want." He made his way to the bathroom.

"That's it fixed do you want to try it?"

"No I fucking don't is that all you wanted me for?"

John turned unable to believe the voice he had just heard, "Christ Almighty! I never thought I'd see you again."

Wilson stared at him and the look on his face told John that although it took a few seconds Wilson realised who he was.

"Bit of a comedown for you, isn't it?" asked John.

"Whatever, it's none of your business."

"Maybe not, but it's good to see you in these circumstances. Nobody deserves it more than you. Justice for the Spaniards you robbed, the churches you looted, the grief you caused others and for plain cowardice. Hopefully your live a long and miserable life."

"Fuck off Bristow."

"I'm just about to. I may go and visit some old friends in Shoreditch. Quite a nice area now they've cleared some of those bomb sites. Some real crooks live around that neighbourhood you know."

"You bastard you had something to with it, didn't you?" His face was a purplish red and he looked like it would explode.

"No idea what you're talking about," John winked, "but if you can't remember what I told you in Italy, Ill repeat it."

John stared at him and Wilson shrunk back, "this is Gods earth and He never put me on it to be fucked about by the likes of you."

* * *

As much as I could have made good use of the monies remaining in the Lloyds Manchester account we had all agreed that theft wasn't part of the deal and the bank was surprised to receive a letter from the USA [posted by Jesus] detailing where the balance had originated and apologising for any loss they may suffer.